OUT TRICKED
AND IN
DANGER

OUT TRICKED AND IN DANGER

HEATHER ELIZABETH
GLOBERMAN

TATE PUBLISHING
AND ENTERPRISES, LLC

Published by Tate Publishing & Enterprises, LLC
127 E. Trade Center Terrace | Mustang, Oklahoma 73064 USA
1.888.361.9473 | www.tatepublishing.com

Tate Publishing is committed to excellence in the publishing industry. The company reflects the philosophy established by the founders, based on Psalm 68:11,
"The Lord gave the word and great was the company of those who published it."

Book design copyright © 2011 by Tate Publishing, LLC. All rights reserved.
Cover design by Christina Hicks
Interior design by Chelsea Womble

Published in the United States of America

ISBN: 978-1-61346-247-8
1. Fiction, Fantasy, Contemporary
2. Fiction, Action & Adventure
11.09.06

This book is dedicated to the doctors, nurses, psychologists, physical therapists, and occupational therapists at the Pediatric Pain Rehabilitation Center in Waltham, Massachusetts. I could not have made it to where I am today without you guys.

And to anyone else out there struggling with Reflexive Sympathetic Dystrophy (Chronic Regional Pain Syndrome), I know it's hard, but don't give up hope. You never know what's waiting around the corner.

PROLOGUE

The train tugged lazily along the tracks as if it hadn't a deadline to make, but the conductor wasn't worried. He'd never been late. Not on the slowest of days. Why would his trustworthy train pick today of all days not to be on time? It wouldn't. He looked out the window and saw the glistening Atlantic coast fly by. A fiery orange sunrise was already beginning to rise up over the ocean to the conductor's left. It was a truly beautiful sight.

That's when suddenly something was wrong. The view out his window suddenly went from the wide array of colors mother nature had to offer to a deep shade a purple in less than the time it took him to blink. The train began to shake violently, as if it'd been caught in the middle of an earthquake, but there weren't any fault lines on the east coast. Then, he knew it was not an earthquake, for the train began to hover off the tracks! His heart leaped into his throat, and his fear held his feet cemented in place.

Before he could register anything else, he realized the train was getting higher as the seconds raced by! Before he knew it, the train was suddenly lifted what seemed and felt like thousands of feet off the track, but there was no way to be sure. Then it felt as if the conductor's stomach was being yanked down through the floor as it fell, until everything was hanging from the nose of the coal-powered old train. The tracks were getting farther and farther away by the minute.

The conductor turned his head to see if he could get sight of what was causing this when he saw something in his peripheral vision. He turned his head and saw the train's cargo was pressing against the door of the car where he was now. The door wasn't going to hold on much longer. He could already see the hinges coming off the wall. And with a loud *clang*, the door broke in half. Something heavy came down and hit the conductor in the head. Then everything went black...

CHAPTER ONE

The shrill sound of Julie's alarm clock awoke her at six forty in the morning as usual. She didn't want to move or go to school; she just wanted to lay there. But not sleep.

Julie yawned, sat up, and swung her legs over the side of the bed. She looked in the mirror that covered her closet wall.

Her long, curly, black hair resembled a birds' nest, and the sunlight that poured in from the window made her emerald eyes shine like polished glass.

Out of all the kids at her school, Julie, Qwin, and Nathan (their older brother) didn't stick out much with Julie and Nathan's dark hair and beautiful eyes and Qwin's sandy blonde hair. Or at least they didn't stand out much on the outside. But on the inside, they had the biggest secret in the world. They were wizards and witches.

Julie crossed the room to her vanity to pick up her hairbrush when suddenly she heard a loud *boom!* She raced out of her room and down the stairs until she stood next to Qwin in the kitchen doorway. The kitchen was a mess! There was shattered glass on the floor and jam, peanut butter, butter, bread and pancake mix everywhere. The toaster stood in flames in the corner.

For a second, Julie stood in shock watching the flames lick the kitchen cabinets.

Then Nathan rushed in, slipped on a piece of bread, and fell flat on his back. The loud thump his head made when it hit the floor snapped Julie out of shock.

"What'd you *do*?" he accused Julie.

"Me? Whatever happened in here, Qwin did it!" Julie cried, pointing at her sister whose mouth fell open in shock.

"Just because something blows up doesn't automatically mean that I had something to do with it!" Qwin defended herself.

"Did you?" shouted Nathan as he stood up.

"No!" Qwin answered.

"Then who—," Julie was interrupted by a groan coming from the corner next to her. She jumped to the side and was about to recite a spell when Nathan interrupted her.

"You can't do the spell! You always mess up and hurt someone!"

The last time Julie had done a spell, she had been trying to levitate a piano. She levitated something all right, but it wasn't the piano. After she had accidentally levitated her brother, she'd had some difficult getting him down…needless to say, her father had to drive him to the ER that night.

All three children were taught there magic from their father. There weren't many magical schools left in the world anymore, and none in Texas, the children's home. So they attended a public school for academics, and their father taught them magic at home. They each had been given countless spell books to use as references, but Julie mainly used hers to keep her furniture level.

"I do not!"

"Yeah, you do."

While they argued, Qwin recited the spell. "Mess up, cleanup!" In a bright flash of light, the kitchen was spotless. They turned toward to the corner where the groan had come from. They saw their dad standing up in the corner. He didn't appear harmed, which was only slightly surprising. Qwin may have been half a decade younger than her older sister, but she somehow managed to go longer than Julie without mispronouncing spells. All three of the siblings were on different levels of magic.

"You tried to make breakfast again, huh?" asked Nathan.

"Yeah," Phil Lynnel answered his son. There was still a piece of toast on his head of short blond hair.

Ever since the kids' mom went missing when Qwin was just a baby, Phil Lynnel had always tried to make them breakfast, even though he never succeeded. He could have used magic, but the thing was, as wizards and witches grew older, the weaker they became. This usually started to happen around age twenty-seven or twenty-eight. Until that age, though, a wizard or witch's powers continued to grow. Their powers actually got so strong that once they got old enough, they had trouble controlling them. For example, when Julie was Qwin's age, she got frustrated with one of her friends and threw a fit. She didn't notice a car that she had been standing in front of at the time had vanished—that is, she didn't notice it until she got home and it was parked in the middle of her bedroom. Incidents like those were the whole reason wizards and witches even bothered to learn how to use their powers. But anyway, Phil was forty-seven. He still had enough magic left to teach his children and perform simple tasks, but he mostly did things the way mortals did, as a way of getting used to the lifestyle. Julie told him countless times that she could do the cooking spells for him, but their stubborn father always refused the offer.

Phil believed that his children needed to learn how to do things the way mortals did, as well, so that they would blend in better with their society. For hundreds of years, magic had been a well-kept secret. Witches and wizards went about in the everyday world, attending schools, using the mortals' technology, but when there were no mortals around, they pretty much used their powers for everything. Sometimes they would use a phone or laptop, but only because they were so used to using one in public.

Julie crossed her arms, shook her head, and returned to her room. She was followed by Qwin, and after a few silent moments of staring at his shoes like they'd suddenly become really interesting, Nathan went to his room as well.

When the children's mother had gone missing nearly nine years ago, Phil had been devastated. She had been a kind witch, a grade school teacher. Nathan had remembered as if it had only been yesterday what had happened; she'd lost her job, first of all. Budget cuts had been bad that year, and the school had been forced to let several teachers go. So Mrs. Lynnel had traveled all over the county and then the state looking for work. Her family had stayed behind in Amarillo. She had opened a communication portal each night so that she could tell her children good night face to face, but one night, her portals stopped coming. After one day, Phil had been worried, and then when two days passed without any word, he became frantic. The Wizard Police had searched for her, but to this day, Amelia Lynnel was still missing.

After Julie was dressed and ready for school, she went back downstairs and poured herself some cereal; then she sat next to Qwin at the table.

Qwin's sandy blonde hair was pulled into a ponytail, and her jade eyes were sad. She wore jeans and a pink T-shirt that said "She Did It" with an arrow pointing to the right across the front.

"Did you have another dream?" Qwin whispered.

"Yeah," Julie whispered in answer. "In this one, a train was lifted—"

She was interrupted by their dad coming in from getting the morning paper. "Hey, guys, listen to this," he exclaimed as Nathan entered the kitchen. "'The *Saleem* (a gold carrying train) vanished off the tracks late Sunday afternoon. Late last night the train was found off the coast of Boston under thirty feet of water! When it was found, it was literally torn to shreds, but the train's cargo, 157 bars of solid gold, was missing along with the conductor, James Hidolyn, and the crew, Joseph Cadle, Forrest Sounders, and Carl Johansson. The police have no idea to how this could have happened.'"

"My dream!" Julie whispered in shock to Qwin. For the past week, she'd dreamed of robberies taking place on planes or airplanes involving people she'd never even met. And the weirdest part was whatever she dreamed came true! The only person she ever told about her dreams was her little sister, Qwin.

Her dad read the last sentence, which worried her the most: "This is only the latest in five gold carrier robberies that have taken place on trains and airplanes."

"I'm going to be late for school," muttered Julie as she dumped her cereal in the sink and grabbed her book bag.

"That makes two of us!" Qwin agreed nervously, although the reason she was leaving had nothing to do with school.

Nathan looked confused. "But the bus doesn't—." He never finished because when Qwin picked her book bag up and swung it over her shoulders, it hit him in the face. "Hey!" he cried angrily.

And with that, Julie and Qwin raced out the front door.

Only a few hours later, Qwin sat in the principal's office of Amarillo Prep, waiting for her dad to show up.

He opened the door and stepped inside, but before he could ask what was going on, the principal handed him a sheet of paper and stated indifferently, "Here's your bill."

"I didn't know I had to pay for my child to attend," he explained.

"You don't. This is for everything Qwin's broken today," said Principal Spence as she shook her head of curly red hair.

Phil looked at the bill in shock and turned to his daughter. "How do you break a ladder?"

"You knock it over," Qwin answered nervously.

"How do you break *your teacher?*" he cried angrily.

"Hit her with a ladder." Qwin smiled.

"This is not funny!" screamed her dad.

"Glad to be on the same page." Principal Spence sighed.

He gave the bill one last look. "Dare I ask? How do you break a computer?"

Qwin smiled her biggest smile yet. "Push a ladder over so that it hits your teacher and she falls backward and breaks the only computer that she can put our math grades in."

"Mr. Lynnel." The principal sighed irritably. "Qwin's suspended."

Just as Phil Lynnel rose to leave with his daughter, the principle's secretary walked in. "Excuse me, Principle Spence," the secretary said, "Mrs. Taylor, Julie Lynnel's reading teacher, has just sent her to the office."

"Qwin, go wait in the hall," ordered Principal Spence. "Mr. Lynnel, sit." Then to the secretary, she said, "Send her in."

Julie waved to her little sister, walked into Carol Spence's office, sat down, handed her a note from her teacher, blew a bubble with bubble gum, and turned to her dad. "You're already here?"

"She normally uses the time it takes for you to get here for executing her escape plans," the old woman explained. "Apparently you came in to Mrs. Taylor's class tardy—for the forty-ninth time. Not only that, but you didn't attend *any* of your morning classes. Why?"

Julie tried to think up a good excuse. "I heard that a fire broke out in my little sister's class, and I wanted to make sure she was okay."

"If you were so concerned, tell us what started the fire," demanded Principal Spence.

"Um…an electrical outlet?" Julie guessed.

"No, it was a computer. Let's try another question. Why weren't you in your morning classes?"

"I...am not a morning person?"

Both Principal Spence and Mr. Lynnel raised critical eyebrows.

"Okay, I stopped by DQ to get a milkshake then went to the movies. Afterward, I remembered I had to go to at least one class today, so I came to this dump."

"*That* I believe." The principal sighed. "Julie is also suspended."

"*Also?* Who else got suspended?" Julie wondered.

"Qwin," Mr. Lynnel muttered as he left the office for the second time that day.

As they walked into the hallway, Qwin stood up. "What's the verdict?"

"Heard you got suspended too." Julie smiled as she gave her sister a high five.

"You two think it's funny? Just wait until we're home!" their dad shouted.

That evening Qwin and Julie were grounded. Luckily there were bathrooms in their rooms, because they weren't allowed to leave them; they couldn't even talk. Their dad brought them food and set up web cams outside their bedrooms in case they tried to leave, which neither girl had the nerve to do. It was supposed to be like that until their suspension was over. But it didn't last.

On the third day of their grounding, Mr. Lynnel called them downstairs. The two girls sat on the couch, and their dad stood in front of them. "Do you know why I called you downstairs before your grounding was over?"

"No," they both answered.

Nathan was sitting in the armchair in the corner watching a baseball game, but he was also listening.

"Yesterday I got a letter in the wizard mail advertising a boarding school for witches and wizards called 'Auroratine' that teaches not only the mortal essentials but also magic."

Julie and Qwin were snickering.

"What's so funny?" Phil cried.

"Okay, that's the dumbest name I've ever heard!" Julie laughed.

"Let's see how funny it is when you're attending!"

"That's weird. For a minute, I thought you said me and Julie were going to that school," Qwin said.

"You heard right," Mr. Lynnel told her. "Your train leaves for the outskirts of New Elder, Connecticut, in two days."

"What?" Julie cried.

"How could you do this to your own kids?" Qwin yelled, standing up. But their dad had already left the room.

Julie stood up, but before she went to her room, she saw Nathan snickering at his sisters while he watched the game. "It's *not* funny!" Julie sobbed.

The next day the girls cleaned out their lockers and told their friends good-bye. Julie's best friend, TJ Tomas, walked past, stopped, and slowly walked backward until he was face-to-face with Julie. He saw she was putting everything from her locker into a cardboard box and shook his head in confusion.

"Hi," Julie muttered miserably.

"Why?" TJ asked.

"Huh?"

"You're cleaning out your locker?"

"Kinda." Julie sighed.

Before she could explain, TJ whined, "But these are your throwing eggs." He picked up a carton of eggs she'd been putting in the cardboard box.

"My dad is sending me and Qwin to some wizard boarding school," she explained unhappily.

Julie could still remember the day she'd found out TJ was a wizard. It had been quite a shock for both of them to be honest; magical families were extremely rare. So rare to the point that the chances of actually having *two* magic families in one town were practically somewhere around one in a million. It had been back when Julie and TJ had been merely seven years old. They had known each other for several years before that and were already good friends.

When they were in the third grade and learning about plants, they had been given a standard project: each was to grow a lima bean plant in a milk carton. The plants stayed in the classroom by the window. Everyone was doing a good job raising their plants, but when it got to be the end of the second week and everyone's was growing but Julie's, Julie had taken matters into her own hands.

When the bell for recess rang, the class of hyper little children stampeded into the hall in such a rush that their teacher, a twenty-four-year-old first-time teacher, hadn't noticed Julie was still in the classroom hiding in the closet that had been used to store book bags. After she left and the room was empty of all except for her, Julie climbed noiselessly out of the old wooden closet and tiptoed over to the window where her milk carton filled with soil sat soaking up sunlight. She grabbed hold of the window sill and rose up on her toes to get a better view and whispered, "Little green plant, tiny and small, grow until you're bigger than them all!" What happened next was not what Julie had intended.

Very slowly, a little green stalk appeared on top of the soil. Just as Julie began to feel an enormous sense of pride, things took a turn for the worse. The little green sprout continued to grow and began to grow faster until the entire front wall of the classroom was covered in little green vines. Julie stepped back and surveyed the damage. "That's not good."

She nearly jumped through the ceiling when she heard a voice behind her say, "Whoa!"

She'd spun in surprise to find TJ standing there, gaping in awe. Her mouth fell open. and her stomach had churned with fear, "TJ? Why are you…Oh, no."

TJ had walked forward until he was at her side, still staring at the mess Julie had made, "Would you like some help fixing this?"

Julie was shocked by his offer, "How could *you* fix this? You weren't even supposed to *see* this!"

TJ had just smiled and said, "Leaves and vines and that grow up and down, wither away and turn to brown." Just like that, in less time than it took Julie to blink, the plant shriveled and turned brown, dying all at once.

Julie was quiet for a long time as she stared at what had once been her project, "You…you're a wizard!"

TJ nodded. He then added, "We should probably clean this up before everyone else comes back inside." And that had been it. There was no more talking about it as if it were some huge deal, even though it was. They were just two seven-year-olds with one more thing in common, one more thing that brought them together.

"Auroratine?" TJ wondered.

"Yeah, you've heard of it?" She turned to TJ after she put a pair of pliers in her box.

"Heard of it? My dad is sending me there!" TJ stated in shock.

Julie wasn't one of those soft people who would shed a tear at a movie theater, or make a big deal out of getting a good grade or even someone's birthday, so you could tell she was happy when she gave TJ a huge hug.

"Wait." Julie paused, stepping back. "Why are you being sent to prison?"

TJ laughed at what his best friend had said. His spiky orange hair was a little messed up in the back from Julie's hug. "I found out from my dad your dad was sending you away, and I thought, *Why be miserable here without my best friend when I could be miserable there* with *my best friend?*"

Julie couldn't help it; she hugged TJ again. Someone walking by saw the hug and snickered. Julie blushed and stepped away. TJ called after the person, "It's not funny."

"I gotta go," Julie muttered, hurrying away.

CHAPTER TWO

The car ride to the train station was painstakingly quiet. Julie and Qwin had sat next to each other in the back seat of their father's beat-up, old station wagon with their book bags sitting in their laps. They had each packed two suit cases, which were piled on top of each other in the trunk of the old, candy-smelling car.

Julie had packed her suitcase full of her favorite magazines and photographs from back when they were still one big happy family: her, Qwin, Nathan, their father, and their mother. She had contemplated packing a few of her own spell books but decided against it. She didn't expect to study; she expected to give the teachers her worst effort. She wanted them to call her father and write so many letters complaining that Phil would get a headache just looking at his mail pile.

Qwin had pretty much packed the same as Julie, only instead of pictures of her family, she'd packed those that she'd had of her friends. Qwin wanted nothing to do with her father anymore; neither girl did.

As Phil drove, he attempted one last meaningful conversation with his daughters. "I'm only doing what's best for you, you know." That got no response, so he tried again, "You'll thank me some day." Had it been nighttime, he'd have been able to hear crickets in the silence that seemed to flood the car. So he tried one last time, "You do know I love you guys, don't you?"

Julie remained sitting stubbornly quiet with her arms crossed in anger, but Qwin spoke the accusation that she would want to take back for the rest of her life, "You don't love us. I bet you didn't love Mom either, and that's why she vanished. No one kidnapped her; she wasn't murdered. I bet she just got tired of your lies."

Julie was dumbstruck by the words that had just come out of her little sister's mouth. *How could she say that?* Their mother would have never just left them! And how would Qwin know anyway? She was only a year or so old when Amelia had vanished. *Qwin was just angry,* Julie told herself, *she knows that's not true.*

But their father was also struck speechless by Qwin's words and Julie began to realize something very unnerving: the car was slowing down. *What have you done, Qwin?* Julie thought.

The car came to a stop in the middle of the barren, dirt road. There was nothing surrounding them but desert. "Dad?" Julie began to worry even more.

"Get out," he ordered.

"Dad—" Julie tried again.

"Out."

The girls climbed out through the right side door and walked around back. Julie helped her sister get her bags out of the trunk. "The train station is one mile in that direction," Phil called to them. Once they had made it to the shoulder of the road, their father made a U-turn and sped away, leaving his daughters standing there watching him shrink into the distance, until they could not see him anymore.

As they stood there staring after him, Julie muttered, "I blame you."

"I didn't know he'd—"

"Qwin?"

"What?"

"Don't ever talk about Mom like that again."

They'd been walking down the road dragging their bags behind them for what felt like an eternity in the scorching Texas heat, when a car pulled to a stop beside them. The passenger window rolled down to reveal TJ smiling at them. "Need a ride?"

"Yes!" the sisters cried in unison. So the Tomas family drove them to the train station.

Upon arriving, TJ pulled his lone suitcase out of the trunk and the headed into the massive train station together.

Amarillo National Train Station had a lobby the size of a football field and a roof that seemed to Julie to arch to equal height as the stadium seats would rise. A golden lamp hung from the ceiling on a matching golden chain that went with the cream-colored paint that covered the walls. The floors were made of a red ceramic tile that echoed every step and sound made in the station. To Julie's confusion, TJ's mother led them past the ticket booth and straight toward the train terminals.

Qwin was equally confused. "What about our tickets?"

Mrs. Tomas turned and handed them each a plain, stiff sheet of paper. Julie's read: Passage for Julian Lynnel Location: (outskirts) New Elder, Connecticut Train Terminal: 45. Qwin's was similar.

They struggled to keep up with TJ's tall, athletic mother as she quickly strode through multiple terminals, "We're taking a train with mortals?"

"No," she explained, "mortals aren't given the option to ride this train."

That statement seemed to even confuse TJ, "Why not?"

"Because it's going to a location that belongs to wizards, so the wizard that controls the train made sure this one didn't appear on the mortal registry."

The group finally came to a halt as they reached a giant iron sign that stated simply: 45. Julie looked to the terminal on her right and took in the massive plaster columns that held up the roof, the giant train that was already parked and waiting for its passengers. A man stood in a blue uniform waiting to take their luggage as the passengers boarded the train; Julie couldn't help but notice all the passengers were children and teenagers.

Mrs. Tomas let out a breath. She turned to her son. "This is it." Julie and Qwin walked toward the train but stopped a few yards away and waited for TJ to finish saying his good-byes. Julie was really starting to wish Qwin had not brought up their mother in the car; then they might have someone to say good-bye to, or at least deny a good-bye to.

TJ quickly caught up with them as his mom waved. "Ready?" Julie nodded. "Let's go."

The train was divided into sections; they were told they could each chose their own. Each section had two benches facing each other. The benches resembled bus seats except for one difference: instead of wrinkled and torn leather, there was a scratchy layer of burlap covering the outside of the benches. Each section had an empty doorway that led into the aisle, which ran down the length of their car. Julie, Qwin, and TJ entered the section they had chosen. At the end of the small room, there was one window bordered by the ends of the two benches. TJ closed the sliding glass door behind them, and they all noticed an overpowering scent of dust and other unnamable things. "I call a window seat!" Julie and TJ called at the same time.

Qwin strolled unhappily over to an overhead shelf that she guessed their luggage was supposed to go on. On the shelf above the seat to the left, Qwin noticed two neat sets of folded clothes. "Aww, man!" she cried miserably.

"What is it?" Julie wondered as she walked to her sister's side.

"We've got uniforms!" Qwin sobbed.

Julie picked up a piece of paper that was taped to the first pile. "That's strange."

"What?" TJ sighed.

"It has all my information on it," Julie explained.

"Must be *your* uniform." Qwin sighed as if it'd been obvious.

"What do you mean information?" TJ questioned.

Julie quoted, "'Julie Lynnel: fourteen years old, five foot four inches, dark hair, green eyes, two siblings, size three and a half." Her eyebrows knitted together in confusion.

Qwin assumed, "They must do it to avoid mix-ups."

"It's still weird," TJ muttered.

Qwin looked at hers: "Qwin Lynnel: ten years old, four foot two inches, blonde hair, green eyes, two siblings, preteens, size five." It was creepy.

TJ walked over to the shelf above the opposite seat. "I see my uniform and information sheet, but there's someone else's too."

"Who's uniform?" Julie asked, crossing the section.

"The info sheet says Zach Forrests's," TJ read, uncertain.

"The train's about to leave," Qwin stated. She looked out the section window and looking at the clock that hung on the egg shell-colored wall of the platform. "I wonder where he could be."

Suddenly someone standing in the doorway to their section cleared their throat, and the trio spun around. In walked a boy TJ and Julie's age. He had brown hair that wasn't too long and wasn't too short. He was tall and slender, and he had devastatingly good looks. "Um…is this section thirteen?"

"I don't know. Did you read the number above the door?" TJ teased sarcastically.

Julie elbowed him in the side and gave him a stern look. "Sorry about him. I'm Julie. You must be Zach."

"Yeah, how'd you know?"

"There are information sheets taped to each of the uniforms on the overhead shelves." Julie smiled.

"Should we go change?" TJ said in a desperate attempt to get Zach away from Julie.

"There's most likely a long line for the changing rooms. Maybe we should wait a little longer," Qwin suggested.

"I don't mind staring at your beautiful eyes a little longer." Zach smiled at Julie as they all took their seats.

As it turned out, not only was Zach a smooth talker who paid most attention to Julie and pretended TJ didn't exist, but he was also a real schmoozer. After an hour on the train, Zach went to change into his uniform.

"I don't like the way he talks to you," TJ grumbled. He slouched angrily in his seat, arms crossed. "And he acts like I don't exist."

"You say that like it's a bad thing." Qwin sighed.

Eventually they all changed into their uniforms. The uniforms were blue sweaters over white button-ups and skirts for the girls and khakis and blue button-ups with white sweater vests for the guys. "We look like clowns," whined Qwin.

"Could be worse." Zach sighed.

"How?" muttered TJ.

"We could have big, floppy shoes and clown hair," Zach joked.

They all laughed except TJ. Julie elbowed him in the side. "Elbow me one more time, and you'll break my ribs." She elbowed him one more time, and he laughed sarcastically at Zach's joke. "Ha ha."

For TJ, the train took all eternity instead of five hours to reach the school grounds. They all climbed off the train and stretched. It was night when the train arrived. The platform was damp and reminded all the kids of an in-ground stage. It seemed ominous and gave them all an uneasy feeling. There were six teachers waiting for them. One was introduced as the dean, Dr. Culbreth, who had short, dark hair and a black beard that ended in a point. His most noticeable feature was his eyes; they were a cold, uninviting gray. They were like steel doors that didn't let anything in or out. In a loud, booming voice he announced, "Welcome, stu-

dents. Please file into five orderly lines behind your professors."
He gestured to a line of five tall, unmoving figures that each wore
their own black, cotton cloak with the hood pulled down low,
obscuring any facial features. "From left to right, their names are
Ms. Faircloth, Ms. Lindsey, Mr. Sawyer, Mrs. Sawyer, and Ms.
Edwards. They will get you all squared away." The professors
took them to the sign-in desks where they got their schedules
and dorm assignments and found out they each would have a
roommate. They were told to find their rooms, meet their roommates, and meet in the grand hall in one hour.

Julie wandered hopelessly through the halls of her new prison.
There was no light in this part of the school except for Julie's candle. She held a crinkled, old map that was yellowed with age. "I
hope I find my dorm soon," she mumbled to herself. The paintings on the walls were of people with unfriendly faces. One portrait was of a woman being threatened by a vampire hunter with
a stake. Like the platform where the train had dropped her off,
something about this painting was giving her a creepy feeling.
Julie stopped to get a closer look when she saw something that
nearly gave her a heart attack. The vampire hunter's eyes were a
cold, frightening gray color, and they were staring straight at her!

She stumbled backward, wondering if she was really seeing
this. But even as she stepped to the side, the eyes of the painted
canvas followed her every move. Scared half to death, Julie raced
down the hall and bumped straight into a familiar figure in a
black robe with a hood pulled down over his head. "No running
in the halls," an indifferent voice ordered.

"S…sorry," Julie stammered. "Can you tell me how to get to
dorm"—she pulled out a sheet of paper and gave it a sideways
glance—"six-six-six?"

The teacher stared down at her, his face hidden by the hood.
The threatening figure pointed in the direction opposite of where
Julie had come from. She started to walk in that direction, follow-

ing the walls. Julie hadn't been walking for three seconds when she found her room on the left side of the ominous hallway. "That's embarrassing," she muttered to herself. "I walked right past it." Then to the man who'd helped her, she said, "Thanks for the—" She paused when she spun around and found there was no one there.

"That's strange." She sighed aloud. Julie pushed the door open and found a brightly colored room with two twin beds. The beds had pinstriped sheets, and there were two vanities on the opposite wall from the beds. And opposite from the door was the white door that led to the bathroom. Sitting on the bed farthest from the entrance to the room was a girl with strawberry-blonde hair. She was very thin and smiled kindly at Julie when she walked in. The girl stood up and crossed the room. She shook Julie's hand timidly.

"I'm Kristine."

Julie smiled in return. Kristine seemed nice enough. "Nice to meet you. I'm Julie. Sorry it took me so long to get here. I got lost. This school must be bigger than Buckingham Palace!"

"I honestly couldn't tell whether or not you took a long time to get here because I got lost as well!" Kristine laughed. "This school is so creepy; it's like a haunted house I once saw at the county fair. The only thing that doesn't give me chills is the dorms!"

Julie agreed, and then a curious thought came to her head. "Did you see that strange portrait only a few yards from our room?"

"Which one?" Kristine wondered sarcastically. "This place must have a thousand of them!"

"The one of the vampire hunter threatening a woman with a stake."

"No, can't say I have."

"You mustn't have gone that far when you got lost," Julie explained. "Let me show you."

Obediently, Kristine followed her roommate out the door of their dorm and a few yards down the hall. Julie was reluctant to go back to the place where she'd had her scare, but Kristen had to see this. Julie really needed to know what she thought. But the weirdest thing happened. When they reached the painting, the hunter's eyes had changed! Instead of the strange gray they'd been earlier, they were a dull purple. "You're right," mumbled Kristine, rubbing her arms gently. "This painting gives me the creeps."

Julie was speechless.

"Come on," Kristine coaxed. "We better hurry, or we'll be late to the grand hall, wherever that is." Kristine took Julie's wrist and tugged her away. And as they left the strange painting, its eyes became aglow with a strange purple light.

Not only that, but during the whole run to the grand hall, Julie had the weirdest overpowering feeling that they were being watched by unknown eyes lurking in the shadows of what was probably the gloomiest school in the United States of America.

Once they ran through the doors of the great hall, they bent over with their hands on their knees, took in a few deep breaths, and took a look around. It was a room larger than a football field! There were windows that started at the ceiling, which appeared a mile above them, and ended on the floor where they stood looking up in shock.

"Wow," Kristine said.

The room was filled with hundreds of kids in uniforms. The room was painted a faded yellow that had once, many years ago it seemed, been the color of sunflowers, and also had mahogany paneling. The room smelled of rose and snapdragons, and the end of the room rose up like a stage. On the stage, there was a long table; behind it were chairs that looked old enough to have been used by King Arthur; each chair was made of wood from a live oak and the backs of the chairs were decorated with an intricate pattern that made them seem somewhat more elegant.

Then, with a puff of smoke that smelled of cherries, the professors each appeared behind chairs, and the dean stood behind the biggest chair. Dr. Culbreth cleared his throat, and again in a voice that it seemed not even thunder could rise above, he announced, "This is the grand hall, as I'm sure, or at least I hope, you can all tell. For the remainder of the year, you will gather here for meals *only*."

Several students were confused by this because there was no furniture that they could see, other than the teachers' table and chairs.

"You will attend your classes every day. There is magical mixtures, taught by Mr. Sawyer. Incantations and magic recourses, which will be taught by Mrs. Sawyer. Ms. Lindsey will be your instructor for defense, magic recreation, and PE. Ms. Edwards will teach math and science, and last but not least, Ms. Faircloth will teach social studies, language, and reading. There will be consequences for those who break the rules clearly laid out in the student handbook, and, but not limited to, bad grades and disrespect. Finally, I'd like to explain to you all that I do not give 'breaks.' Everyone will be punished for every infraction, every time."

To Julie, none of this seemed like a shock. When he was done, in his loud, frightening voice, he recited a spell, "Appear, food for all, here, in the hall!" With a flash of blinding light, a buffet table longer than an Olympic swimming pool appeared, and on it was more food than Julie had ever seen in her life. Next to the table were several piles of plates and silverware that were stacked high in piles taller than she was! Not only that, but as students started to line up and serve themselves, more of whatever they took just reappeared right before their eyes!

"I so need to learn that spell!" Julie cried in awe.

"You're not alone," Kristine agreed. "Are we supposed to just eat on the floor?"

Julie shrugged. At the moment she was so stunned by the buffet table that she really didn't care if they ate on the floor or even outside.

They found Qwin and plopped down onto the hardwood floor next to her and her roommate, whom she introduced as Lacy. She was short and very thin. Lacy had her medium-length brown hair in a ponytail, and she seemed extremely nice. She and Qwin were bunking on the other side of the school, which, apparently, had lighted hallways, unlike the wing of the school where Julie and Kristine were living.

They talked and laughed and ate until they were stuffed and exhausted. The feast in the grand hall lasted three hours, and around ten o'clock they all headed back to their dorms. Kristine and Julie discovered their room was at the end of the hallway, not that they could've found out on their own because all they could see, even with a candle, was a shower of darkness.

That night, as Julie lay in her bed dreaming, she saw the cargo of five hundred bars of gold. "This is the pilot of plane 714 requesting permission to land." The pilot was currently flying through a cloudbank. In response to his message, a voice cracked on the radio, "This is the Louisiana tower. You have permission to land on runway twelve." The pilot lowered his plane out of the cloudbank and into the icy night. The gold bars, in groups, were flowing from the cargo hold and through the walls of the plane, but the pilot didn't notice.

A voice from the tower contacted him over the radio for a second time. "The lights on the runway are out, so we're going to bring you down. You are two hundred fourteen feet off the ground."

The captain brought the plane down a few more feet. He had no idea he was about to lose his life. "Roger," the pilot answered the instructions. The tower called over again, "You are one hundred fifty feet off the ground." The pilot brought down the plane a little more. "One hundred feet of the ground," reported the tower. "Fifty feet," the person at the tower had been lying, but the pilot had no way of knowing he was being lied to. He brought the plane down, and suddenly he was face-to-face with the concrete. His plane crashed, resulting in the biggest explosion Julie had ever seen. The smell of smoke filled Julie's nose and mouth. She coughed and choked on it. Suddenly she was wide awake. But the smoke didn't go away.

She shot straight up and blinked a few times. She stared around the room and saw no fire or smoke, but the smell lingered. Julie leaped from her bed and shook Kristine awake. Kristine groaned and woke up. "It's three in the—," She paused and looked around then jumped from her bed, nearly knocking Julie over. "Is something on fire?"

"I don't know. I don't see a fire, but I can smell one for sure," Julie explained in a rush.

"I have a flashlight in my dresser," Kristine said. "I'll get it, and we can check the hallway."

Kristine raced to her dresser and got her flashlight. The girls burst into the hall and shined the light in the direction of the other rooms and found nothing. They spun around and faced the end of the hallway and saw smoke pouring from the eyes of the vampire painting. Then as if someone had flipped a switch, the smoke vanished and took the smell with it.

CHAPTER THREE

Julie and Kristine tried as hard as they could to forget what they'd seen the previous night, but the image of the smoldering painting was burned into their brains. They couldn't fall asleep again that night, and they showed up to class sleepy and jumpy. They couldn't tell anyone; they knew that for a fact. Besides, who'd believe them? Julie had asked Qwin that morning at breakfast if she had seen or smelled anything strange last night, but neither Qwin nor Lacy had had any odd experiences the previous night.

"So you guys didn't like, smell anything weird or anything?" Julie had pressed.

"Smell anything like what?" Qwin wondered.

Julie had hesitated and then slowly confessed, "Smoke?"

Qwin's eyes grew wide, "What'd you set on fire?"

"Nothing!" Julie insisted, and that had been the end of it.

Julie walked to her table in the center row in the front in her magical mixtures class. She plopped down in her stool next to TJ. The classroom was on the first floor of the south wing of the school. Julie had only been in a small part of the south wing, but she could tell it was in bad need of repair. There were shattered tiles on the floors of the halls, and entire portions of the plaster walls were missing. The classroom itself had a ceiling that sagged awfully low and looked like it could collapse at any moment; in addition, it had water dripping from the ceiling. Support beams kept the room up and also made it look like a giant mine. There was one long table in the front of the room, and behind it stood the ingredients cabinet.

"You look terrible!" TJ cried when he saw Julie.

"Thanks, because, you know, that's the first thing a girl loves to hear in the morning," grumbled Julie, propping her head up on her hand.

"Sorry, Julie. I didn't mean to—" TJ began to apologize.

"I know. I know. I look terrible. The beds in this place couldn't be any harder to sleep on," Julie lied. Lying to TJ made her uneasy. He was her best friend, and she had never fibbed to him—not once. However, Julie just couldn't bring herself to try to explain the incident from the previous night. TJ would think she had been just dreaming, and maybe she had. Though Julie knew it had not been a dream; Kristine had seen it too, and not even wizards and witches shared dreams.

"I guess," TJ muttered, unsure. "Hey, there's something I really have been meaning to talk to you about since the train ride—" Again TJ was interrupted.

Mr. Sawyer walked into the class, hood down, and for the first time, the class saw his face. He was an old man with so many wrinkles that if Julie had a dime for every one of them, she'd be rich. He had thin, white hair and hands that looked covered in shrink-wrap. He had old, gnarled fingers that were curled tight in a ball as if he was mad. "Take your seats!" he ordered angrily.

Julie recognized his voice from her first night when she'd asked directions. He strolled briskly to the front of the room and started to call roll.

TJ slipped Julie a note that read, "Julie, you don't really like that Zach guy, do you?"

Julie read it and quickly scribbled a reply onto the notebook paper, "Heck, yeah!"

Mr. Sawyer was still calling roll when he called out a name that caught both TJ and Julie's attention. "Zach Forrests?"

The two turned in the direction that the answer had come from and saw sitting at the table next to them was Zach! He sat next to Kristine, and he was smiling at Julie, who blushed.

"I hate that guy," TJ muttered to himself.

Suddenly the roll call was over, and the teacher announced, "Today we will be working on a simple yet useful mixture. It is known as the 'belief' mix because it gets the person who ingests the mixture to believe anything that the brewer of the mix says." Mr. Sawyer went on to tell them more about the mixture, such as how it was developed by their very own Dr. Culbreth. "Now the ingredients to make this are spread out in front of you, and we will be making a small sample today." They looked at the various plants and elixirs spread out in test tubes and petri dishes across their tables. "The ingredients needed are three crushed roses, two leaves of a snapdragon plant, a teaspoon of liquid sulfur, and just a dash of powdered newt eyes."

He demonstrated how to make it, and everyone in the class made a perfect sample, but they weren't allowed to keep them. At the end of class that day, all the samples were taken up. TJ and Julie were too busy quietly arguing about Zach to notice that Mr. Sawyer neglected to take up Zach's sample.

The bell that signaled it was time to switch classes rang all too late for Julie because it gave her just enough time to get TJ blazing mad at her for defending Zach every time TJ pointed out one of his flaws and not apologize before it rang. Julie walked angrily up the stairway and into the school hallway. She raised her schedule to her face and sighed unhappily. Her next class was spells and magic resources. Suddenly Zach was next to her.

"Hey, Julie."

"Oh, hey, Zach. What's your next class?" Julie smiled at her best and tried to forget she'd lied to TJ. She was unsure why, but that still bothered her.

"Spells and magic resources," Zach read. "And here it is." Zach stopped and pointed to a door to his left.

"I have that class next too!" Julie said. "You must have telepathy, because you can find your way around the school so well."

Zach held the door open for Julie. "Something like that." Zach laughed, and they found seats next to each other at a table in the back.

Mrs. Sawyer strolled angrily down the aisle made by the first and second rows of tables. She had silver hair and so many wrinkles she could have been a waitress at Jesus's last supper. Her hands were well folded into fists. Her gnarled fingers were longer than her husband's, though. She stood behind a podium, her thin figure nearly hidden by the center of the podium. She started to call roll and then began to teach the class.

"Today, in the category of spells we will be working on what I like to call 'spell improvisation.' For instance…" She strolled over to a table that stood to her right. On it there was a leaf she must've picked from the back garden. "Silence in dark, give me a singing lark!" And with a strange purple glow, the leaf turned into a singing bird! "I made that spell up, but if it rhymes and if doesn't repeat words you've already used, it's a 'made-up spell.' But keep in mind," she said as she crossed the room and released the lark through a window that she left open a crack, "just because it is called a 'made-up spell' doesn't mean it isn't a spell. Now, you have an assortment of objects in front of you. I will go around the room alphabetically, and in order, you will each create your own spell, and I shall assess it. But do not hesitate, or I will take points away from you for every second it takes you to think." She looked at the attendance sheet. "Now, Abigail Cooper."

"It's Abby," corrected Abby.

"One, two, three," Mrs. Sawyer started to count all the seconds Abby had hesitated.

Abby focused on a test tube in front of her. "The fun I need to join, give me a gold coin!" With a flash of white light, the test tube turned into a one-dollar gold coin.

"That was my best test tube!" Mrs. Sawyer screamed. "Principal's office, and you get a negative three on that spell."

"So...a ninety-seven?" Abby guessed.

"No!" their teacher yelled. "A negative three. Now to the principal's office, *Abigail.*"

And with that Abby climbed off from her chair and trudged out of the room. Mrs. Sawyer picked up the coin and slid it in her pocket after Abby had left. "Now," Mrs. Sawyer continued. "Morgan Clifton."

Morgan closed his eyes so he wouldn't give away what he was focusing on, "As the room filled with fog, Will turned into a frog!" The room suddenly filled with fog, and there was a loud *bang*! Everyone coughed and choked then waved the fog away. Mrs. Sawyer turned on the fan, causing the fog to clear, and they all saw that Morgan had turned the person sitting next to him into a frog!

"Zero," the teacher announced. "Also, I forgot to mention, you have detention!" Then a flash of purple light appeared. The light had left a detention slip personally signed by Mrs. Sawyer. Then she crossed the room and picked up a jar of orange dust and sprinkled some over Will. With a loud *croak*, Will was back to normal. There was a series of "ahhs" and "whoas" from the class. "This is *erase dust!* You will learn about this in magic resources," she announced. "Now." She looked at her clipboard and announced the next student to demonstrate a spell. Soon they were in the Gs and then the Fs. "Zach Forrest."

Zach took a deep breath and focused on a dead leaf that had flown in from the window. "This leaf is now not; a seed of blooms should fill its slot!" And suddenly the leaf grew smaller until it was a seed. And then the seed split in half, and from it grew a tree, and from the tree grew flower buds, and from the buds bloomed the most beautiful flowers any one had ever seen.

The teacher was speechless. Everyone in the class clapped and whooped; even the teacher was clapping uncontrollably. "Well done! Well done! A plus!" The teacher took her clipboard out and put down Zach's grade.

The teacher kept going through the class roll until it was Julie's turn. "Hurry up," Mrs. Sawyer barked. "The sooner this is over, the sooner I can swap out classes for one with kids who don't turn their lab partners into frogs."

Julie sighed. She'd been thinking about what she'd do while everyone else had been presenting their spells. Their rhymes had come so easily for them. Julie had a headache already. "Um... Teacher, thou art mean. Go to ... the bottom of a ravine!" Suddenly in a flash of white light, the professor vanished. "Oops."

"What should we do now?" Zach wondered, staring at the spot where Mrs. Sawyer had been.

"We should probably tell Dr. Culbreth *someone* sent our teacher to a ravine," Morgan suggested.

"Or we could end class early," suggested Zach.

"I like your brain." Julie smiled. And with that, they all filed out of the room to explore the school.

"My brain says thanks." Zach smiled.

Meanwhile, TJ was in his PE, flight, and magic defense class. Today, they were flying brooms, which was what TJ was worst at. It was like TJ picked the worst possible school to attend, and he was seriously reconsidering staying there for Julie, considering it would seem that she could probably get along fine now that she met Zach.

"TJ Tomas," Ms. Lindsey called, "could you please, for five minutes, *please* hang on to your broom!"

TJ was in the flight part of the class, and TJ had fallen off his broom twelve times in the past hour. His head was aching from multiple goose eggs, and he was pretty sure he at least sprained his wrist. "After how Julie treated me in our last class, she doesn't deserve my being here," he grumbled. "And that Zach jerk is starting to rub off on her," he worried to himself.

Ms. Lindsey blew her whistle. Everyone turned to see she was speaking to someone on the watch-sized communication portal she wore on a leather strap around her wrist. "What?" From what they could hear of the conversation, something was wrong. She hung up and turned to the class. "A student in the spells and magic resources class used a made-up spell to send Mrs. Sawyer to a ravine somewhere in the world. While I'm gone, you are all to go to the grand hall and wait for further instructions. Also, the students from the class that has a missing teacher are running around the school and disturbing other classes. If you see the following students . . ." She started to called names from a sheet of paper she'd used to take notes on during her phone call. When she called the name Zach Forrest, TJ smiled. *It'd be so fun to finally see that kid get sent to the dean's office,* he thought. He could still remember what the dean had said yesterday about how he didn't give breaks. Then Ms. Lindsey called out a name that filled him with worry: Julie Lynnel.

Oh, no! If Julie is caught, she'll probably get in big trouble. But, why should I care? She's been so mean to me! Well, I guess I really provoked her. Maybe I should've given Zach another chance. When he saw her again, he needed to apologize, but above all things, he needed to make sure she wasn't caught. But there was still one thing that bothered him. Had Julie sent their teacher away? *Let's see ...teacher goes missing; it's a student's fault—yeah, Julie did it.*

He walked with the rest of his class to the grand hall. On the way to the hall, there was a long stretch of hallway so long and with so many windows that it'd earned the name Window Lane. The left side of Window Lane overlooked the east garden of the school. Even though the east garden was extremely beautiful, all students were forbidden to go there. There was not even an entrance to that part of the school that the kids were aware of.

There were two main reasons why the kids couldn't go back there: (a) That was where the teachers grew ingredients for the potions class, and they didn't want the kids to get their hands on dangerous things, or at least that's what they told them, and (b) they could access the Headless Woods. The Headless Woods were rumored to be the home of giants, trolls, and living skeletons. Most kids were pretty sure the teachers just said those existed to keep students out of the woods—ogres, fairies, unicorns, and river serpents. Now, some of the occupants of the Headless Woods sound nice, but they aren't.

Unicorns, which are portrayed as nice, friendly creatures, didn't eat plants; they didn't eat animals either. They ate *humans*. As for the fairies, they weren't much different from the unicorns. The would lead children who wandered into the east garden toward the woods and put them into a trance, then they would skewer the child and cook them over a campfire. Some said the fairies were in liege with the headless hag. The headless hag wasn't really headless, though. She was an evil, old witch who lived deep, deep in the woods. They say that she would slay the children the fairies brought her and use their magic powers to keep her young. Everyone was pretty sure that was a lie to keep them out of the woods, like the skeletons. Although, there had been some kids who had gone missing in those woods.

"Hey, you want to buy a newspaper? We're selling the local papers from the nearest town to raise money to buy ingredients for charms," a kid standing in the middle of Window Lane next to a paper rack said.

"Here, dude." TJ smiled tiredly, handing the kid two quarters. He gave TJ a paper, and his eyes widened in shock at the headline. Somehow incorrect data had come across from the control tower at a Louisiana airport, causing a cargo plane to crash and causing the biggest explosion in Louisiana history. But when they had examined the wreckage of the plane, its cargo—five hundred bars of gold—wasn't even remotely there. Not even a micro piece was there! It was like the gold had never been on the plane. TJ's eyes were even wider with every line he read.

"Something wrong?" the paper kid questioned.

"No, no," he muttered.

TJ started walking again, and as he walked, he looked out the multiple windows in Window Lane. He stopped. *Is that…No, it couldn't be.* He squinted and snaked his head out the window to get a better view. *Yeah, that really is Zach walking through the east garden! But who is that walking with him?* It certainly wasn't Julie. The girl he was holding hands with was a blonde. TJ watched as they walked straight into the Headless Woods! He half considered going after them but decided that whatever happened, Zach deserved it. And that girl he was walking with probably deserved whatever she got too. But he couldn't help but wonder who she was.

TJ shook his head and started walking again to the grand hall.

Qwin and Lacy had been in Ms. Faircloth's class learning about things she thought she'd never use in real life, such as the fact that a wizard's power was at its full height during the new moon, when Ms. Faircloth got an interesting call on her own portable communication portal, which was identical to Ms. Lindsey's. They were sent to the grand hall so that the teachers could hunt down a bunch of kids who sent their teacher to a ravine in some unknown part of the world. So there they were. Qwin and Lacy were sitting in the southeastern corner of the room texting each other:

Who do you think sent the teacher away?

Let's see … What grade did the teacher teach?

Ninth.

Julie. It was definitely my sister.

Just as she was sending this, Julie walked over and plopped down by her sister. "What're you doing?"

Qwin jumped in shock. "Aren't you supposed to be terrorizing the school or something?"

"Well, you see, my classmates and I were going ice skating, but someone turned up the heat at the local rink and melted the ice, and so we just came back to school to prank everyone else's classes. But when we came back, we found everyone in the grand hall and the teachers freaking out in the teachers' lounge," Julie said. "Zach and I were going to use a spell to keep the teachers off Mrs. Sawyer's tracks, but I lost Zach in a crowd."

"Well, if you're lucky, the teachers who were freaking out in the teachers' lounge won't find out that you sent Mrs. Sawyer to that ravine." Lacy sighed as she put away her phone to join the conversation.

"How did you know *I* did that?" Julie cried in shock.

"That was a guess," Lacy explained.

"Which was apparently accurate." Qwin smiled, putting her own phone away.

"Well, it was an accident," Julie admitted. "But she had it coming."

"From what I've heard, she did indeed," Lacy agreed.

"I heard you had a lot of fun in spells and magic resources today," TJ said as he sat down, placing the newspaper he'd bought in Window Lane next to him.

"Geez! Number one, it was an accident! Number two, she— wait! How many people know about this?" Julie cried in anger. "By the way, I'm sorry about what I said earlier."

"Me too," TJ apologized. "I guess I kind of provoked you anyway."

"Right now I just want to forget about school," Julie mumbled.

"Okay, then," TJ agreed. "I know how much you like to hear about current events." TJ referred to how often Julie had checked to see whether or not her dreams or nightmares had come to life. Of course, he didn't know that was the real reason Julie was always listening to the news and reading the paper. Julie felt uncomfortable, maybe even a little embarrassed about the dreams, for she had no idea why she was having them. So she stuck with telling her little sister, who never made snap judgments.

"So I bought you this newspaper from a stand in Window Lane."

Julie tried to hide her eagerness as she snatched the newspaper. The story nearly killed her from shock, even though she had partly expected it.

"Dude, you okay? Julie? Julie? Guys, I think there's something wrong with Julie! She's white as a sheet!" TJ shook Julie gently by the shoulders. Qwin and Lacy crawled up next to Julie and started to nervously call her name.

"What's going on?" Kristine wondered as she crossed the room from where she'd been standing.

"There's something wrong with Julie," TJ cried in worry.

"I'll go get the nurse!" Kristine rushed, but just before she left, Julie snapped out of it.

"Uh, sorry. What were you saying?" Julie shook her head to get the room to stop spinning.

"Julie." Lacy sighed in relief. "What happened back there?"

"I...uh...that happens whenever I go into shock," Julie explained.

"It's true," TJ verified.

"What shocked you?" Qwin asked, already having an idea that it had something to do with Julie's nightmares.

She handed Qwin the newspaper. Lacy and Kristine read over her shoulder. "Whoa," they all mouthed.

"Oh, and by the way." He was going to love seeing the look on Julie's face. "Zach has a girlfriend."

Lacy, Qwin, and Kristine dropped the newspaper, their mouths open.

Julie turned to him in frantic desperation. "How d-do you know?"

"I saw him walking with her and holding hands with her in the east—" He broke off his sentence. If he'd told them the east *garden*, they would have never believed him.

"Oh." Julie sighed in disappointment.

"Wait!" Kristine cried, pointing her finger at the floor like she saw something "Was the girl a blonde?"

"Yes," TJ answered. He didn't like where this was going.

"That was Abby! She doesn't even know who Zach is! I was just talking to her a minute ago, and she said she wanted to see the headless hag's cottage, but once she and the guy who was showing her where it was got into the woods, they got lost and came back," Kristine explained with relief.

And that was the end of the worst day for TJ. But one thing was still there pecking at the back of his mind: *How the heck does Zach know where the headless hag's cottage is?* And then came another thought: *How does Zach even know that there is a real headless hag?*

"Where is this Zach guy anyway?" Lacy questioned. "I've heard so much about him from Qwin, but I've never met him."

Suddenly the giant table appeared, along with all the chairs. And then, just as before, food appeared on the table with a bright flash of light. They all stood from their place in the corner and looked around. There wasn't a teacher in sight who could have recited the spell.

CHAPTER FOUR

Julie and Kristine woke up that morning to find their door locked from the outside and a note on the floor. It read:

Dear students,

Many of you are unaware that when you send a person to an unknown place in the world, the person must know where they are in order for them to use magic to return to where they were originally. Some of you were already aware of this, but we felt the need to tell you so you'd know why it's taken so long to recover Mrs. Sawyer.

We'd also like you to know whoever sent the professor away is in an unbelievably large amount of trouble, and as soon as we discover who the culprit is, they will be sentenced to detention for the rest of the year.

Today we are proud to announce we have recovered Mrs. Sawyer, though she hit her head and doesn't remember who sent her away. In order to give her some time to recover, there will be no school today. Enjoy it while you can.

Lastly, you may wonder why your doors are locked. We don't trust you to roam the grounds unsupervised, so you will be stuck in your rooms for the remainder of the day. Food will be teleported in. *Anyone* caught roaming the school grounds will be sent to my office.

I hope I made today's ground rules clear.

Dr. David Culbreth

Kristine let out a whistle. "You better pray they don't realize it was you."

"Okay." Julie shrugged. "In the meantime, this room has no power—"

"What are you doing?" Kristine asked nervously.

"Take me to the east tower!" And with that, Julie vanished in a blue light.

Mrs. Sawyer was walking through the east garden picking eglantine flowers for a charm she was running low on when suddenly she had that weird prickly feeling she always got when someone was watching her. She spun around and searched the garden; then she turned to the east tower, but even though she strained her eyes as hard as she could, she could find no one else around. She told herself she was being paranoid and continued collecting ingredients, but as the prickling sensation increased, she decided to go inside. As she walked along the cobblestone path back to the building, she decided to pick ingredients another day. Then, out of nowhere, something blue and gooey fell and hit her smack on the head. Her hand reached up and pulled the sticky object off her head. *A cupcake?* She looked up and saw Julie Lynnel leaning over the edge of the second highest window in the tower holding a water balloon the size of a bowling ball.

"Bomb's away!" she yelled as she dropped the water balloon. The water balloon busted the second it hit Mrs. Sawyer. But there wasn't water in the balloon; it was syrup.

"Young lady, you are in so much trouble!" Mrs. Sawyer threatened. Suddenly Julie disappeared into the tower. The old lady huffed angrily and started walking again. Suddenly she spotted Julie leaning out a window just above her head. Julie suddenly dumped a pillow filled with feathers over the ledge, and with that, Mrs. Sawyer looked like a giant chicken.

She raced into the building, and just before Julie could use her powers to poof away, Mrs. Sawyer grabbed her arm and escorted her to the dean's office.

When Mrs. Sawyer walked in holding Julie by her elbow, she looked so much like a mad chicken, Dr. Culbreth actually smiled. "Is something wrong?"

"This child is a menace!" Mrs. Sawyer shouted at the top of her lungs.

"Why do you think my dad sent me away?" Julie asked sarcastically.

"I want her expelled!" Mrs. Sawyer screamed, continuing her tirade.

"I thought I made it clear in the note that going outside your rooms was strictly prohibited," Dr. Culbreth said, narrowing his eyebrows.

"No, you said getting *caught* was strictly prohibited," Julie corrected.

"It doesn't matter!" Dr. Culbreth barked. "I said all the same, and you deliberately disobeyed me."

"Get over it," Julie muttered, propping her feet up on his desk.

"Get your feet off my desk." He growled. "And furthermore, since I have more important things to deal with today, I'll just give you detention five times a week for six weeks. And if I ever catch you in my office again, you'll be expelled."

"Whatever," Julie muttered.

"You are really pushing it today, young lady," snapped Dr. Culbreth.

Mrs. Sawyer suddenly looked like she remembered something. "Later, I think the teachers need to discuss something important."

Julie and Morgan were in detention the night after that. The detention room was a small, windowless room with no doors. The walls were a dark green, and a fireplace stood against the front wall. It smelled like a fire had happened recently, and it must have been a hundred degrees in there. The floor was made of squeaky hardwood like the rest of the school. There was one square table in the middle of the room just big enough for two checkerboards, lengthwise anyway. Julie sat down in one of the only two chairs in the room. It was placed directly across from the chair where Morgan sat. No teachers had been placed to watch them, and they were given no work to do.

"What are you in for?" Morgan asked, thinking they'd discovered she'd sent away Mrs. Sawyer.

"Got caught sneaking around yesterday. Well, I honestly wasn't sneaking, because I purposefully dropped a cupcake on Mrs. Sawyer's head," she explained with a small smile at how funny she'd thought that the cupcake had been. "Why did you turn Will into a frog?"

"Because I couldn't think of a spell. I mean, I was trying really hard, but..." His voice trailed off.

"You weren't thinking. You were sleeping with your eyes open," Julie accused, narrowing her eyes at him.

Then a voice came across the loudspeaker, "No talking in detention."

"How did you know? That I was lying, I mean," Morgan whispered.

"Because your eyes twitch when you lie," Julie nonchalantly answered. She stood up and crossed the room to a wall. She rapped on it once with her fist and then moved on to another section of wall and repeated the motion.

"Have you lost it?" he whispered in panic.

"No, the teachers said that the students' magic doesn't work in here. When they put us in here, they walked us in while we were blindfolded. They didn't poof us in, which mean they're saving their powers for something else, and they probably don't intend to poof us out." She moved on to another section of wood and rapped on it once then moved on. "But we students have to get in and out somehow, which means there is a secret passage somewhere. Now help me look," she ordered as she switched to a different wall.

Morgan stood up and started searching the wall across from her. "That actually makes sense." He stopped talking and tapped the walled three more times. "Does this sound hollow to you?"

Julie moved over so that she was next to the wall and she could hear well. She tapped it three times and then began to scan the floor.

"What now?" Morgan whined.

"Look for a lever or button, something to open it with," she ordered.

"Wow, you must really hate detention," Morgan reasoned as he helped her look. "You don't exactly come across as someone who likes thinking."

"This is common sense," Julie explained. "Got ya." Julie saw a part of the floor that seemed secluded from everything else. It was off in the corner, and the wood was cut to make the shape of a strange square. Julie waltzed over to the wooden tile and stepped on it. At first nothing happened, and then after Julie put her weight on it, there was a loud rumble, and the room began to shake. The part of the wall that Julie and Morgan had decided was hollow fell away, revealing a passage that existed in between the walls. "Yes!" Julie cheered.

"You're amazing, but you overlooked one little detail," Morgan pointed out.

"What's that?" Julie frowned.

"How are we gonna clean this up?" Morgan cried, gesturing to the wall.

"That's not important." Julie recovered quickly. They stepped into the hallway, and somewhere off in the distance they could hear the faint sound of water dripping. Julie felt her way along the cold, stone wall because the darkness hid the way. Julie did her best to watch her step, but it seemed no matter where she or Morgan stepped, they seemed to be stepping in a puddle. Suddenly Julie's hands could not find the wall. "I think that there's a turnoff."

"But the wall keeps going on this side," Morgan observed, feeling the opposite wall. "We should keep going. I don't think we've gone far enough from the detention room." They kept walking for a few minutes when Morgan found a second turnoff. "Should we go this way?"

Julie was about to agree when she heard voices coming from farther down the path they'd been following. "Wait, listen." Julie and Morgan stood quiet for a minute. "Come on. We're going this way." Morgan followed Julie down the passage they'd started on and toward the voices. Finally they came to the end of the hallway.

"It's a dead end. We should have gone the other way," Morgan complained.

Julie felt along the wall that made the end of the hall and found what felt like a latch. She pulled back on it, and a small opening appeared. "Morgan, wait!"

He turned around and walked to Julie's side and peered into the opening. When he turned back to Julie, he had an excited look on his face. "It's the teacher's lounge!"

Julie shoved him over and looked through the hole. "They're talking about us!"

"We can't cancel the trip!" Ms. Edwards insisted. "It's a tradition! We can't cancel it because of two *children!*"

"Well, we can't leave them unattended. They could escape!" Mr. Sawyer objected.

"Here's an idea," Ms. Lindsey interjected. "Take them with us."

"No!" all the teachers except Dr. Culbreth yelled in union.

"Not a bad idea," Dr. Culbreth admitted.

"Where do you think they're taking the class that we can't go with them?" Julie wondered as she moved aside to let Morgan peek through the hole.

"Sir, you're not actually considering it?" Ms. Faircloth pleaded.

"Doesn't matter where they take the class," Morgan muttered. "If the school year keeps going in this direction, you and I and every non-nerd in this school will end up having a terrible time anyway."

"Yes, I am. They're coming with us, and that's final," Dr. Culbreth declared.

"But, sir—," Ms. Edwards started.

"Gail, who is the dean at the school?" Dr. Culbreth questioned as he stood up, ready to leave.

"You," all the teachers mumbled.

"And don't you forget it," Dr. Culbreth warned. "Now, go get those kids out of detention."

Julie slammed the latch shut. "We have to get back to the detention room!"

"What? I thought the whole idea of sneaking out was so that we could *escape* detention!" Morgan cried as he followed Julie as she ran as fast as she could back to the detention room.

As they reentered the detention room, Julie explained, "No. That was so that we could spy on the teachers." Julie frantically looked around the room for a way to hide the wall. "How'd the teachers hide that?" she gestured to the crumbling wall.

"It's called teacher's magic. Something we don't have!" Morgan panicked.

"The table!" Julie cried as she raced over to the table.

"What about it?" Morgan screamed.

"Help me move it in front of the wall!" Julie ordered.

Morgan crossed the room until he was helping Julie with the table. "And what's our story? That the window was open and the wind blew the table up against the wall? Oh, yeah, there are no windows in here!"

"Yeah, that story works," Julie agreed.

"I was being sarcastic!" But they didn't have any more time to argue, because as they returned to the middle of the room, Ms. Lindsey poofed in.

She stared at the table in shock. "What happened?"

"A gust of wind came in from the window and blew the table up against the wall," Julie nervously lied.

"What window?" she demanded. "Doesn't matter. The sooner you get back to your rooms, the better. The students are going on a campout in the west garden tomorrow night. I suggested that you two stay back to prevent trouble, but since there are no teachers allowed to stay back, you two have to go."

"So that's what they were arguing about!" Morgan whispered.

"Huh?" Ms. Lindsey asked, turning to him.

"Nothing."

Julie frowned. "I hate camping."

Ms. Lindsey scowled. "Well I hate you, but I'm stuck with you anyway."

"Why do you guys have a camp out anyway?" Morgan pondered.

"Because the wizards who founded this school thought the students deserved to have some fun at the beginning of the year. *Obviously*, they didn't have to put up with you two." And with that, they were led back to their rooms.

The camp out was announced the next morning, and the majority of the students were surprised to hear about it at such short notice. As they sat Indian style on the floor of the grand hall finishing breakfast, Dr. Culbreth explained, "This campout is mandatory. No one will stay behind. After your last class at four, you will each be sent back to your dorms to gather your necessities, unless you are a tenth, eleventh, or twelfth grader, in which case you will conjure up what you need as part of this morning's incantation warm-up.

"Those of you who go back to your dorms will be there no longer than thirty minutes. Then you are to meet in your first period classroom. Your teacher will be waiting for you. He or she will escort you to the west garden and show you where you are to set up your tent. Each student's tent will be in the same designated area as the rest of their class. You *will* share a tent you're your roommate. No exceptions. If you are in the tenth, eleventh, or twelfth grade, you will go straight back to your first period class from your last class, and your teacher will escort you to the west garden from there.

"No one will leave their designated class area. The teachers' tents will all be on the right-hand side of the garden. No students are to come near the teachers' tents.

"There will be a bonfire, and dinner will be served there. There will also be a campfire story, to which you *will* pay attention. I hope I've made myself clear."

"Wow," Lacy raised her eyebrow, "A campout? Where did that come from?"

"They've been planning it since before we got here," Julie answered.

"Did I miss something?" Kristine turned to Julie, confused. "How do you know that?"

Julie blushed and realized she hadn't mentioned what she and Morgan had found in the detention room or even what they'd heard; Kristine was already sleeping when Julie had returned to their dorm, and Julie had been too exhausted herself to try and wake her. "Morgan and I were in detention last night," Morgan looked up from his plate of scrambled eggs as if hearing her for the first time. Julie continued, "And we found a hidden tunnel in the wall."

"Cool!" Qwin exclaimed.

"Lower your voice!" Lacy hushed her. "I'm guessing secret means the teachers didn't want them to know!"

Julie picked up in a quieter voice. Everyone leaned in to hear her over the din of the other children, "We followed it all the way to the end, and there was a latch built into the wall. I opened it and saw it opened into the teachers' lounge. They were talking about the campout...they didn't want to take Morgan and me." She smirked at the last sentence; at least she knew that the teachers were already fed up with her, so it shouldn't be long before the calls and letters home began.

"Why?" Kristine started to ask but then her mouth opened wide in realization. "They thought you guys would be trouble."

Julie nodded and she smiled wide then. "I intend to be." Julie sat herself down in the weeds and watched as Kristine and the two other kids they'd be bunking with for the night (luckily, they had been assigned Qwin and Lacy) struggled to get the tent up. The giant, navy blue, nylon tent continued to collapse on top of the three girls over and over again, pinning them to the ground. From Julie's point of view, it looked like they were wrestling with the tent, and they were losing. Several times, she broke down and laughed at them.

"A little help!" Kristine beseeched her.

"In a minute!" Julie would always shout in response as she laid out lazily on the ground.

"It's been a minute!" Qwin finally screamed in frustration.

Julie had simply shrugged and said, "In two minutes."

Once or twice she'd picked up a rod they were looking for and tossed it their way, but she almost always nailed someone in the head. After this happen the third time, Kristine finally yelled as she rubbed her forehead where the rod had hit it, "That's it! Quit trying to 'help'!"

Finally, after a half hour of trying over and over again to simply put up the tent, they three girls who'd actually been working got it to stay. They stepped back to admire their work. Julie rose from the ground and joined them.

Julie sighed. "I didn't realize that putting up a tent was so much work."

"How would you know?" Qwin muttered sarcastically. "You didn't do any of the work."

"I helped you find a few rods that hold up the tent."

"She's right," Lacy admitted. "But you could have done more work."

"Whatever."

The four of them looked around the large field or, as the teachers called it, the west garden. The kids didn't know why they called it a garden. Besides the weeds, there were no plants in the west garden, just a bunch of untrimmed grass. The kids were allowed to wear what they wanted to the campout because the teachers didn't want them getting mud on their uniforms. Julie wore jean cutoffs and a T-shirt, much like her little sister and friends. Julie climbed to her feet and stretched. The left side of the west garden was covered in tents, and the right side was empty all except for the huge pile of wood where the teachers were starting the campfire. The west garden was bordered on two sides by the Headless Woods, which encircled the school. Kristine stood up next to Julie. The tall weeds tickled their legs.

"I liked detention better," she mumbled. "I'm gonna see if TJ has his tent set up yet." And with that, Julie walked off into the crowd of tents.

"I'm gonna go see who Abby's sharing a tent with," Kristine called to Qwin as she too walked away.

Lacy looked around confused, "I thought we weren't supposed to leave our designated…Oh, what the hey," And with that she stomped off to find her own friends.

Kristine walked past tons of tents until she saw Abby's roommate, Kelsey, sitting alone in front of a tent near the end of the field. Kelsey looked so sad and quiet. That wasn't like her. She was normally so happy.

"Kelsey!" Kristine called. But Kelsey couldn't hear her over everyone else's excited chattering. "Kelsey!" she repeated. But her cries fell on deaf ears. She finally made it to Abby and Kelsey's tent. "Kelsey!" Kristine yelled in Kelsey's ears. Kelsey nearly jumped to the moon.

"Oh, uh, hey, Kristine," she greeted her unhappily.

"Is something wrong?" Kristine questioned with worry. "I called your name twice."

"Oh, I just…Am I mean? Or unpleasant to be around?" Kelsey demanded.

"Heck no! Who told you that?" Kristine cried.

"Well, no one. It's just…well, Abby—"

"Wait. Abby told you that? You're great to be around, and it isn't like her to tell lies like that. Or tell lies at *all*," Kristine puzzled. "When did she say that?"

"You should have let me finish. Abby didn't say it, but when school ended yesterday, I went back to our room, and Abby wasn't there. I decided not to wait for her to do my math homework. We normally do our homework together, but that's beside the point.

I couldn't find my pencil, and I knew that Abby kept her extras in her drawer, and I thought she wouldn't mind if I borrowed a pencil, but when I looked in her drawer—"

"There was a piece of paper that said you were unpleasant?" Kristine guessed.

"No, but that's just it, Kristine," Kelsey sobbed. "There wasn't anything! No clothes, no books, nothing. I searched the whole room for her stuff, but there was nothing. I waited for hours for her to get back from class. But she never did. I got so worried I went to Dr. Culbreth and asked about Abby, and he looked up her enrollment and said that her parents called her back home!"

Kristine's mouth fell open in shock. "Abby went home? Why?"

"I don't know," Kelsey whispered through tears. "She just left. She didn't even say good-bye. Do you think it was my fault?"

"No, I'm sure you had nothing to do with it. What did Dr. Culbreth say exactly?"

"He said that Abby's parents called him and said that they needed Abby at home. So she left on a train at noon," Kelsey finished.

"Wait. That's impossible," Kristine cried out.

A confused look crossed Kelsey's face. But before Kristine could explain, a long whistle cut thought the air. "All kids to the campfire area. Dinner is about to be served!" Dr. Culbreth's loud voice boomed out over the crowd once more.

"I guess they're serving us the old-fashioned way," Kelsey mumbled, and before Kristine could explain why she'd said that Abby's parents calling her home was impossible, Kelsey got up and walked over to the right side of the garden to get in line for dinner.

Later, the kids were all seated around the humongous campfire eating their dinner. Kristine had lost Kelsey in the crowd, so she just sat down next to Julie, Qwin, Lacy, TJ, and Zach. "So, TJ," Zach started, "I hear you're having some trouble in flight."

"And?" TJ rudely demanded.

"I'm pretty good at flight, and I was just thinking maybe I could help you out," Zach offered.

"That's so sweet of you." Julie smiled.

"No, thanks," TJ spat. "Julie is way better at flight than you could ever be, and she's helping me in flight."

"I'm all out of punch," Julie cut in. "Zach, could you get some more?"

"Sure." He smiled as he took her cup and went go get her some more punch.

"What is wrong with you?" Julie snapped at TJ. "He's just trying to be nice! Please lose the attitude. The whole point of the campout is to have fun."

"Look, you know you don't believe that this campout was because the teachers wanted us to have fun any more than I believe that escargot was meant to be a delicacy," TJ accused.

"I know, but it is nice to dream," Julie admitted.

TJ tilted his head in confusion. "Why are you acting weird?"

Now it was Julie turn to look confused, "Huh?"

"Hey, guys. Not to interrupt your polite conversation, but there's something really important you guys need to know," Kristine informed them. "I was talking to Kelsey earlier, and she said that—," Kristine was interrupted by Zach taking his seat next to Julie as Dr. Culbreth stood up and thundered.

"Students, quiet down!" he ordered. "Take your seats. We have a very special treat for you, children. Your history teacher, Ms. Faircloth, has a story for you that has been handed down for generations that she would like to share with you. So without further ado, Ms. Faircloth."

Ms. Faircloth stood up with Dr. Culbreth, and her voice took on the same booming amplitude as Dr. Culbreth's as she began. "Thank you, Dr. Culbreth. And he's right, you know. This really is a special story. It goes back a very long time, back to the medieval time. There was once a very old man who was one of the most powerful wizards of all time, and his name was Merlin. He had very strong instincts, and with this in mind, one day he felt a dark presence flooding through the kingdom, and Merlin became very worried. And just as he was going to call for the audience of King Arthur, Merlin was called to his side. He told Merlin of a strange man who came from a faraway land and had requested the hand of his daughter, which meant that the man would be the new king. King Arthur assured Merlin he had denied the man's request, but in response to the disappointment, the man had threatened King Arthur would rue the day he made this unwise decision.

"The man swore that he would send a plague of evil across the land until his request was granted. Merlin asked the king if the man had indeed done as he said, and King Arthur was upset to admit that the man had indeed followed up on his threat, and a villager had reported that the day after the man had come, a plague was spreading through the kingdom, and that very morning one man had already died. He begged Merlin for advice, and Merlin explained that if the man died, the plague would be unattached and vanish. Both King Arthur and Merlin were uncomfortable with the idea of killing a man, so they looked for other options. Merlin decided that their best bet at the moment was to force the man to retract the plague.

"So King Arthur sent his best knights to the place where the man said he lived. Word was sent that while in the midst of the perilous climb up the cursed mountain he lived on, his knights had perished. So the king sent more knights. And they too perished. The king was in a bind. And with each dying villager, the king grew more grief stricken and soon became ill. So Merlin made the decision that he would attempt the journey. So he packed provisions, extra clothes, food, and his all-powerful spell book. Legend says that the spell book is so powerful that if it fell into the wrong hands, the world would only consist of evil and corruption.

"So Merlin set out on his trip. He traveled for days up the mountain through perilous quarries and dangerous woods until finally he was two-thirds of the way to the summit. And with all the villagers suffering and dying below him in mind, he pushed on, determined to reach the top. On the seventh day of his hike to the summit, he saw a middle-aged man stumbling down the mountain. When he asked what the man was doing on the mountain, the man said that he was on his way home from a faraway kingdom. Merlin asked if he had seen a house of any kind when the man crossed the summit. The man said that he had seen a hut, but he also saw a squirrel cross into the yard, and the second it did, the squirrel died. Merlin could see that had a problem on his hands and continued traveling thought the night.

"Soon a hut came into view as the midnight sky turned pink. Only Merlin could see the protective charm that surrounded the house. He pulled out his spell book and used another charm to remove the first and proceeded into the yard. He knocked on the door three times, and when no one answered, he knocked it down. When he entered, he found the man sitting in his den. He looked shocked to see someone in his house, but his shock was quickly replaced with anger, and he used black magic to attack Merlin. The black sorcerer was far more powerful than Merlin, and Merlin's strength was soon depleting. Merlin was on the verge of death, so he took out his spell book, and the magic from the book radiated into a bright white light. And as the vines of darkness tried to wrap itself around the wizard, on contact with the book, the darkness withered away. The light from the book combined with the power of Merlin destroyed the black sorcerer and saved the kingdom of King Arthur but left Merlin in a fatal state. And during his descent down the mountain, he died. When he died, he had his spell book with him. No one ever found Merlin's body or his spell book. And even though it's been thousands of years, some people are still looking for Merlin's book of spells." Ms. Faircloth finished with a bow. There were multiple standing ovations and tons of questions.

There was one question that caught Julie's undivided attention, and it was from Zach. "Is the book powerful enough to reincarnate the darkness that was destroyed that morning?" he wondered.

"Impossible to say," Ms. Faircloth admitted. "But some people believe so."

A little while later people were still asking questions when Zach pulled Julie aside. "So you want to go for a walk in the Headless Woods?"

"The woods are off limits." Julie sighed as if it were obvious.

"Since when has that mattered to you?" Zach teased.

"Sure." Julie smiled.

But just before they could go, Kristine pulled Julie aside. "We need to talk. Listen—"

"Zach and I were just about to go for a walk in the woods. Why'd you have to ruin it?" Julie whined.

Kristine grabbed Julie by her shoulders and shook her as hard as she could. "Let me finish what I'm saying for once in my life! Abby's *gone!*"

"Gone where? To the bathroom? Honestly, do I look like I care?"

"No, gone as in gone home!" Kristine didn't understand her roommate's reaction. She wasn't acting like herself.

"What?" Julie cried as she shook Kristine's hands off her shoulders. "Lucky! When'd she go?"

"No. It's just that something is seriously wrong!" Kristine screamed through tears.

"Why? Because your best friend left without a good-bye?" Julie snapped. "News flash! People do that!" Kristine slowly sat down in the grass with tears running down her face. Julie sank down beside her. "I'm sorry, Kristine. I really didn't mean to go that far."

"Kelsey said that when Abby didn't come home from school, she got worried and went to Dr. Culbreth. She said that he said her *parents* called and said that they needed her at home. But the thing is, Abby's parents died three years ago. She's been living with her grandma, but her grandma had a heart attack and died. She didn't have anywhere else to go, so the Supreme Wizard Counsel sent her here." Kristine sobbed. "That's how I *know* something's wrong! And yes, because she left without saying good-bye. People do that, but Abby doesn't."

"Let's go ask Dean Culbreth about this." Julie took Kristine's arm, and the two stood up. They left Zach standing on the edge of the tree line alone. They walked to the far end of the right side of the field where the teachers set up their tents purposefully on the wrong side of the garden.

When Mrs. Sawyer saw them nearing, she coldly demanded, "What do you want?"

"To speak with Dr. Culbreth," Julie stated proudly.

"No, you can't go to detention for the rest of the year instead of sleeping out here."

"That's not what this is about," Kristine butted in. "We need to see him about a student. It's an emergency."

Mrs. Sawyer put her book down and stood up. "Okay, Kristine. What did Julie do to you?"

"Nothing! You know what? Forget this!" And with that, Kristine and Julie shoved Mrs. Sawyer on the ground and went straight up to the biggest tent and went inside. "Dr. Culbreth, we need to talk to you!"

Dr. Culbreth was sitting in the center of the tent reading a book. He looked up in surprise. "Don't you knock?"

"It's an emergency," Julie cried.

"I don't want one peep out of you, Julian," he barked.

"I thought 'Julian' was a boy's name," Kristine giggled.

"Shut up," Julie demanded under her breath.

"You said this was an emergency." Dr. Culbreth yawned, taking off his reading glasses.

Kristine straightened up. "It is. One of your students is missing."

A serious look crossed his face. "Who?"

"Abby. I mean Abigail Cooper," Julie corrected herself because she knew that he only responded to kids' full names.

"I know what this is about." The dean sighed. "Children, Abigail was called home by her parents, and that's that." He put his glasses on and continued his book.

"But Abby doesn't have any parents!" Kristine poured out.

He ripped his glasses off and dropped his book. "What? I will look into this at once!" The girls couldn't tell that he didn't mean it.

"Thank you." Julie and Kristine sighed in relief.

They stepped out of the tent and found themselves face-to-face with Mrs. Sawyer.

Meanwhile, TJ sat by his tent in an angry slouch. He had seen Zach walk into the woods with another girl. He thought about following him but changed his mind. He wondered where Julie was. He suddenly saw smoke coming from the woods. *Who else could be out there? How close were they to a town?* he thought. He could make an escape. When no one was looking, he slipped into the woods and did his best to follow where the smoke was coming from. He found himself going off trail and down a hill covered in the usual blanket of dead leaves.

After hiking through the woods for a long time, he saw the cottage that the smoke was coming from. He sighed in disappointment that it hadn't been a town. Suddenly, TJ took a step toward the cottage to get a closer look. The smoke wasn't just coming from the chimney like he'd thought; it was pouring out from under the door and the windows. The house was on fire!

"Hello?" TJ called toward the house. He tumbled down a hill until he was in the yard of the tiny home. "Hello? Can anyone hear me?" He thought he heard a cough coming from inside the house. TJ raced forward and grabbed the doorknob. His hands jumped back on contact. The knob was burning hot! TJ brought his leg up and kicked the door as hard as he could, but it didn't break. "Can anyone hear me?" he desperately screamed. There was no answer.

TJ kept trying to break the door in, but he soon inhaled too much smoke and had to retreat to the hill he'd stumbled down earlier. He couldn't see any fire on the outside, or at least not yet anyway. TJ soon fell unconscious from breathing in too much smoke.

The next morning he woke up to the sound of Julie and Kristine arguing. What are they doing out here? He was afraid to open his eyes but opened them anyway and couldn't believe what he saw. He was in his tent! He sat up and looked around. Apparently Morgan and the other boys he was sharing a tent with had woken up and packed up. The tent was empty all except for TJ, his backpack, and his sleeping bag. How did he get back here? He could see Julie and Kristine's outlines outside the tent.

"Fine!" he heard Julie yell. "We'll see what TJ thinks." Julie unzipped the entrance to TJ's tent. "TJ, we need your opinion on something." She saw TJ in his pajamas sitting up in his sleeping bag. "Did you just wake up?" she accused as she and Kristine entered the tent.

"Yeah, I guess," he mumbled sleepily.

"Julie, he just woke up. Maybe we should ask Zach what he thinks instead," Kristine suggested.

"No, it's okay." He sighed. "What'd Julie do?"

"Why do people always automatically assume it was me?" Julie complained.

"Because it was you!" Kristine uncovered.

"What happened?" TJ cried.

"Okay, so we found out that Abby was missing, and so we tried to go to Dr. Culbreth, but Mrs. Sawyer stopped us, and Julie shoved her on the ground, so now I have detention!" Kristine said.

"(A) You helped shove her over, and, (B) detention isn't that bad. You get to spy on the teachers through a secret passage that they don't guard well enough," Julie explained. "It's not that bad. I don't see why she's trying to blame me anyway for something that was mostly her fault."

"My fault!"

"Yes, because if you hadn't said anything about Abby, then I wouldn't have even been there!"

"And who put that idea in your head?" Kristine screamed.

"Zach!" Julie answered. "And if he said it, it must be true."

"I suddenly think that Kristine is right," TJ stated.

"But, TJ..." Julie whined.

"Sorry, Julie. I've got to get ready," TJ mumbled.

And for a moment, Julie had never felt more alone. She left his tent and walked alone back to her tent. Kristine had gone to find Kelsey. She walked, head down, to her tent, and when she was a few yards away, she bumped into someone. "Oh, my bad. Oh, hey, Zach." She smiled as she looked up and saw she had bumped into him.

"What's wrong?" he asked.

"Nothing," Julie said.

"Okay, well, whatever it is, it'll be okay," he assured her. Zach looked at his watch. "Oh, I gotta go. See you later?"

"Definitely." When Julie got back to her tent, she saw Qwin packing her last bag.

"I heard that you got in a fight with TJ," Qwin started when she saw Julie coming. "You okay?"

"I'll be fine." She smiled.

Morgan and Olivia, his girlfriend, were walking near the tree line where there were less kids hanging around. "That Zach guy is so polite. He brought me some more punch last night when I ran out. And what did you do? You sat there and talked to Seth," Olivia complained.

"Speaking of that Zach guy, did I see Kelsey walking thought the woods with him?" Morgan asked as he kicked a rock.

"Nope." Olivia smiled.

"How do you know?"

"Because Zach said you didn't, and if he said it, it must be true."

"I'll see you later, okay?" Morgan slowly backed away, and when Olivia wasn't looking, he broke out into a cold-sweat run. When he reached his tent, he dove in and caught TJ packing his bags. "Dude, there is something wrong with the girls!"

TJ looked up from his duffle bag and turned to Morgan. "So it's not just Julie?"

"Ever since the campfire dinner last night, Olivia is suddenly basing all her decisions on what Zach says!"

TJ turned all the way around, leaving his bag behind him. "I know! Julie too!"

"Something is seriously wrong with this Zach guy, and I plan on finding out exactly what it is!"

CHAPTER FIVE

Before they could say anything else, Mr. Sawyer's voice inquired from the opening of their tent, which Morgan had neglected to close behind him. "Are you ready to go? We're only staying out here five more minutes, then either you come inside, put your overnight bags back in your dorms, and head to class or you could stay out here and get eaten by the creatures that live in the woods. Your call."

TJ jumped upon hearing Mr. Sawyer's voice. How long had he been there? TJ nervously stammered, "I'm ...almost done."

"Good," the old man grumbled, and as quickly as he had appeared, he vanished.

Morgan shook his head as he reached over to where his bag was lying by TJ and snatched it up. He had no sooner flung it over his shoulder when he said, "I'm starting to think the way the girls have been acting isn't the only thing that's creepy around here."

TJ zipped up his bag and clambered clumsily out of the tent, followed by Morgan. The two turned and gazed at their tent with disdain. "Do you know any spells that put away tents?"

Morgan shrugged. "I barely know a spell on how to transfigure an empty plate into a ham sandwich. TJ raised an eyebrow. "My dad's not a good teacher, okay?"

TJ settled with that answer and stepped toward their tent. "Let's just figure out how to take this thing apart."

"Apart?" Morgan mumbled under his breath, "We barely got it together."

To the boys' surprise, taking apart the tent was a lot easier than putting it together, that is, when the pieces weren't flying all over the place and hitting them in places where no one would want to be hit. Just as they got all the separate parts of the tent taken apart and laid out in the grass, Mr. Sawyer materialized once again out of nowhere. TJ and Morgan had been crouched in the grass about to start packing up what had once been a tent when the teacher cried out with frustration from his place behind them, "Oh, for goodness sake! How hard is it to put away a stupid tent? That's it. Move over!"

TJ and Morgan happily stepped aside. Mr. Sawyer reached out his hand toward the ground where the tent pieces lay and recited, "Pick up, put up!" The pieces suddenly shot up a few yards off the ground and began to soar all through the air. The two boys watched in amazement along with several other students who'd been standing around as the bag that all the pieces went in rose up off the ground and opened wide, gracefully welcoming the plastic rods and nylon cloth that flew straight inside it. When all the pieces were in, the bag's drawstring seemed to pull shut on its own, and the bag collapsed back into the grass. TJ and Morgan were still staring at it in awe when Mr. Sawyer barked, "What are you two staring at? We don't have all day! Gather your things and follow me."

The children did as they were told and gathered their things, then followed Mr. Sawyer and the other teachers over to the stairwell that opened back up into the school. TJ felt like one of those little ants marching along the sidewalk; he was in one long straight line of kids just following orders from some old guys... not that he'd ever call the teachers that to their faces.

As they marched up the spiral staircase and into the school, he could hear Mr. Sawyer saying, "Go to your rooms first, then you will all head to the grand hall for breakfast and continue on with your normal class schedules. Any questions?" They reached the landing in time to hear him boom, "None? Good. Now off you go."

The day seemed to drag on forever; TJ and Morgan were both anxious, for they had already decided what they would do. Morgan had friends here he had already known for long periods of time; he insisted to TJ that they could be trusted. Not that that comforted TJ. He recently learned that his roommate's parents had sent him away because it was either that or juvie…again. This fact made TJ seriously stop and wonder just how Morgan had come to know these boys, but it didn't matter. TJ had a bad feeling about his school, and not the normal "I don't like this place feeling," but like he just knew something bad was going to happen, and he feared that if he was too picky about who he trusted, he may not have enough people on his side to stop whatever was going to happen. So he and Morgan decided to create a sort of "task force" to figure out just what was going on.

TJ and Morgan divided up the list of boys they'd put together at breakfast while Julie and Kristine were in the buffet line; TJ passed a note that had his and Morgan's room number on it along with a time to meet there that night and instructions stating specifically "Don't get caught" to half the kids. Morgan would take care of the other half.

Getting the notes to each boy was nerve-racking for TJ. He would slip it in their binder when they weren't paying attention or risk detention by passing the note while the teachers were in the middle of a lecture. TJ wanted oh so desperately to just teleport the note into their folders or pockets, but unfortunately, being only a ninth-grade wizard in training, he didn't know how.

But finally in his fourth period, he passed his last note. Now all there was left to do was wait. It seemed like an eternity had come and gone, but finally it was nighttime. Time for the meeting the he had been so anxiously awaiting all day.

"Okay," TJ began. He was in his and Morgan's bedroom, along with the seven other boys they had so carefully passed the notes to. TJ and Morgan had picked these boys for their task force specifically because, like Morgan and TJ, girls who were close to them had started acting strange. Eight of the boys were sitting on the ground while TJ stood pacing back and forth in front of the white board they had conjured onto the wall. He held a yardstick and kept hitting the palm of his hand with it. It was well past curfew, and if the seven other boys were caught in someone else's room, they would be in huge trouble, but they didn't care. The boys were trying to piece together the reason behind the girls' strange behavior, and they didn't have much. TJ stood to the side and used the yardstick to point at the white board. He had written all that they knew about the night of the campout—in other words, the night they believed the girls started acting strange.

"Let's review what we know." He sighed. "Julie, Olivia, Kelsey, Andrea, Alyssa, Mattie, Elizabeth, and Holly were all given refills of punch by the suspect, Zach Forrest. Does anyone disagree?"

"I have a question," Garret interrupted. "Did you ever consider this guy was just being polite? And that they all started acting weird only moments after they drank the drinks he got them coincidentally?"

Patrick hit him upside the head. "Dude, stop spending so much time with Andrea."

"May I go on?" TJ sighed.

"Yes." They all groaned.

"Abby Cooper went missing only the day before the campout. Eyewitnesses say that she was involved with the suspect before her disappearance. Do we have any new information on the subject?" Silence was his only answer. "Kelsey Dickerson was seen walking in the Headless Woods with the suspect. I will not ask if any disagree because I know that you, Adam, strongly think that it wasn't Kelsey. I would love to tell you that you are right and I am wrong, but you have no proof supporting your theory, so I must ask you to refrain from objecting."

"All I'm saying is Kelsey knows the woods are off limits. She's always been a stickler for the rules," Adam explained.

"Which is why this meeting isn't about the *normal* behavior of the girls. It's about the *strange* behavior of the girls," Hudson shot at him. "Now, TJ, please continue."

"Thank you, Hudson. The last thing we know is that Julie seemed completely unfazed by Abby's disappearance by morning, which is unlike Julie," TJ finished. "She was more concerned about whose fault it was that she had detention—again. She believed that it was Kristine's fault just because Zach told her it was. In conclusion, we basically know nothing except to watch out for Zach." TJ had to squint in the dimly lit room to see clearly. "Adam! Are you *texting* someone?"

"I'm trying to text Kelsey, but she isn't texting back." He shrugged.

"Maybe because it's two in the morning, and she, like every other person in this school, is *asleep!*" Jacob insisted.

Adam just shook his head and put his phone away.

"Look, I care about Alyssa and the other girls as much as the next guy." Max Char yawned. "But we have school tomorrow, and we should probably all head back to our dorms before one of our roommates wake up and realize we're gone."

"You're right, Max." TJ nodded. "We will keep our eyes open tomorrow and report anything suspicious we see at the eleven o'clock meeting tomorrow night. Everyone in?"

They all nodded, and everyone but TJ and Morgan exited into the hall. Garret speed walked, trying not to make a sound as he raced back to his dorm. The halls were so scary at night. A chill slipped down his spine. He heard the sound of a rusty metal flap squeeze shut somewhere in the darkness, which only made him walk faster. Suddenly he bumped into someone, and something wet spilled all over his front.

"Oh, I'm so sorry!" an unfamiliar voice fretted. He looked up and saw the prettiest girl he'd ever seen. Her curly blonde hair fell down past her shoulders, and her blue eyes sparkled in the light of her kerosene lamp. She tried to wipe the water off his shirt with a napkin. "I'm so sorry!" she repeated.

"No problem." Garret smiled kindly as he stepped back and wiped the remaining ice water off his sweater vest. "What are you doing out here this late?"

"I got thirsty so I went to the kitchen for some water. You?" she questioned as she bent down to pick up the plastic cup the water had been in.

"On my way back from a friend's," he admitted. "Are you going to turn me in?"

"Not if you promise not to turn me in," the girl flirted. "I'd better get going."

"Me too." Garret sighed as they started walking in opposite directions to get to their dorms. Garret spun around and called to her, "Wait! I never got your name!"

The girl spun around and answered, "Salfira."

Garret yelled his name, but he couldn't tell if she'd heard him. He watched as the light from her lantern slowly faded into the distance. He realized he'd been holding his breath and let it out in one long sigh. He spun around to go back to his dorm and bumped into another person. He looked up praying it was another student, but as he looked up, he realized he didn't bump into another student; it was Mr. Sawyer. "Young man. You are in huge trouble."

"Uh-oh," Garret whispered in fear.

"Uh-oh is right." He growled. He looked around as if making sure that no one was watching. "Come with me."

Mr. Sawyer dragged Garret by the elbow through the corridors until they entered a giant circle. Every few feet in the circle there was a new hallway, and the ceiling seemed thousands of feet above their heads. They took a hallway to their left, and Garret found himself being dragged through the hallway where all the classrooms were. Garret stumbled down the well-worn hallway behind Mr. Sawyer. Just as the hallway took a hairpin turn to the right, Mr. Sawyer stopped and violently flung open the door to a classroom on their left. A room opened up before Garret as Mr. Sawyer continued to pull him through the door, and he recognized it as Mr. Sawyer's classroom. The teacher dragged him to the front of the room, and there he finally let go of Garret's elbow. Garret rubbed his elbow where Mr. Sawyer's icy grip had been and watched him as he walked behind his table and opened his ingredients cabinet. He shoved a bunch of things aside and pulled out a bottle. He turned around so Garret could see. The bottle wasn't very big, and there were only a few drops of red liquid in it. "Do you know what this is?"

"No, sir," Garret politely answered. The liquid sure looked like he'd seen it before, but where he'd seen it he couldn't recall.

"This is some of my personal stash of belief mix," he explained.

"You must be so proud?" Garret guessed. He wasn't sure what this was about or what he was supposed to say.

"Let's start with a simple question. What are you doing up so late and still in your uniform?" He scowled.

"Just getting something to drink," Garret lied.

"You're lying," Mr. Sawyer accused.

"How did you know?"

"None of the students know where the kitchen is, or, to be more frank, this school doesn't have a kitchen to get water from. Here's another question. Why is it that when I went to bed earlier, this bottle was filled to the rim with a fresh batch of belief mix?"

"I don't know, sir," Garret repeated.

"Let's see. Could it have anything to do with the fact that you smell like you've been rolling in this stuff?"

"What?"

"Belief charm has a distinct smell that any *smart* person would recognize a mile away," Mr. Sawyer challenged.

"What's this about?" Garret asked, raising his voice.

"A cup of belief mix was stolen from my personal stash an hour ago, and I think we both know that you took it. You spilled it on yourself, so I probably won't have to worry about you slipping it in someone else's drink, but heed this warning: if I *ever* catch you in my ingredients cabinet again, not only will I report you to the dean, I will personally make certain you are expelled!" he threatened.

"Look!" yelled Garret. He was extremely tired and irritable; plus he hated it when he was accused of things he didn't do. "I didn't take your precious mix! Okay?"

The two heard a yawn and turned around. They saw Salfira groggily stumble up to the doorway of the classroom, rubbing her eyes and looking confused. She now wore a nightgown and robe and looked like she had just woken up. "What's all the racket?" She yawned.

Mr. Sawyer scowled at both of them. "To your dorms!" He growled, but to his aggravation, only Salfira began to back up. "Now!"

And with that, the two kids fled the room. After Garret made it back to the other side of the school where the boys' dorms were located, he looked around but could not find Salfira. He thought as he walked. Garret started to try and put the pieces together. *So someone stole a mix that can cause the person who ingests it to believe whatever the brewer says, and it had happened during the boys' meeting.* He, for some strange reason, smelled like belief mix. *How is that possible? Could my roommate have done it and spilled some in my dresser? No, the theft only happened an hour ago. One of the boys from the meeting? No, the meeting started an hour before the robbery.* He couldn't think of any reason why he would smell like belief mix. *Unless…No,* he told himself. *Salfira seemed too nice…and yet, there was no other conceivable way he could smell like belief mix. But could Salfira have really stolen the mix? And if she did, why?*

"This school is just too weird," Garret muttered.

Then he decided to do what he should have done in the first place. He used magic to teleport himself to his dorm. He was the only person he knew, it seemed, that thought to look a head in their spell books and teach themselves how to teleport instead of just waiting for their parents to get around to teaching them. Once he got there, he sneaked past his sleeping roommate and into the bathroom. After he closed the door, he took the cup next to the sink and rung out his sweater vest. It was too dark in the bathroom to see what color the liquid was. He still didn't know why Salfira would have stolen the mix, but then an idea came to him: *Mr. Sawyer could have been lying about me smelling like belief mix!* It seemed reasonable to him, considering the fact he had plenty more reasons to distrust Mr. Sawyer than he did Salfira; there was no proof she had lied to him…except that there was no kitchen in the school. The more he thought about it though, he had every reason not to believe her. Plus he had to clear his name, but there was nothing he could do now. He slipped out of the bathroom and into his bed. The second his head hit the pillow he was out cold.

The next day Julie and Kristine were friends again and were both once again worried for Abby.

Their classes were over, and they were supposed to be studying together, but Kristine couldn't focus. She was too fearful of what may have happened to Abby. Julie lay stretched out on her stomach on her bed with a magic resources textbook open in front of her, but Kristine was pacing back and forth furtively in front of the bed.

"Kristine?"

Kristine just continued pacing.

"Kristine!"

"Huh? What?" She finally stopped pacing and looked up.

"Erase dust was invented in ten twenty-three by?"

Kristine's mind raced, but she just couldn't bring forth the answer. "I don't know! Julie, I'm worried!"

Julie pulled herself into a sitting position on her bed, "I can see that. You're wearing a track in the carpet." Kristine frowned and looked down at the ground where she'd been pacing. Julie stood up and walked over to her, gently placing her hand on her shoulder and leading her over to the bed where she sat her down and then took a seat next to her. "I'm sure she's all right."

"Then where did she go?"

Julie's own mind was now racing, trying to think of a believable lie that would make Kristine feel better. "Maybe…I guess she could have been adopted, right? That's what happens to kids who have no one, isn't it?"

Kristine stared at the carpet miserably and responded in a hardly audible voice, "She had me."

Julie shook her head at her own poor choice of words, "But you can't legally be a legal guardian so maybe…Was she ever in foster care?"

Kristine shook her own head slowly, "No. The Wizards' and Witches' Child Service wanted to try here first."

Julie's shoulders slumped; this was not good. "Let's go see if Dr. Culbreth knows anything, okay?"

Kristine nodded soberly, and Julie had to help pull her up off the bed. After a few more words of assurance, Julie led Kristine into the hall and toward the office.

They were on their way to Dr. Culbreth's office to ask if he'd looked into the matter. Kristine knocked on the door as they reached the lobby outside the office. The lobby was small and smelled, in Julie's opinion, like old people. The back wall was lined with red velvet chairs, and the front wall had nothing but Dr. Culbreth's door and an empty receptionist's desk with enough cobwebs to make a wedding dress.

"Come in," their dean called from behind his office door. The two girls entered and took two seats in front of the desk. "Yes?"

"Do you know anything about Abby?" Julie and Kristine questioned him in unison.

"Who?" Dr. Culbreth barked.

Julie rolled her eyes. "Abigail Cooper?"

"I'm sorry to tell you this, girls, but no one with that name has ever attended this school." Dr. Culbreth sighed irritably. "And if that's all you have to ask me—"

"What do you mean? Only a few days ago you told her roommate that she'd gone—"

"Girls, if this is some prank—"

"Wait!" Julie cried. "Call Abby's roommate, Kelsey Dickerson, up here! She'll tell you!"

"One, you don't tell me what to do, and two, if I, the dean, say she probably never attended here, I'm probably right. If you, the students, say she did, you're probably wrong. Three, Kelsey Dickerson was called home by her parents yesterday," Dr. Culbreth hissed. "Is there anything else you would like to rant about?"

"Us? Ranting? It's you who's ranting!" Kristine yelled as she stood up.

"Out of my office!" Dr. Culbreth barked.

"But—," Julie pleaded in a desperate attempt to find out more about Kristine's friend as she stood up.

"Out!" he screamed, pointing at the door.

"Yes, sir," Julie moped. She took Kristine's elbow and dragged her out of the office. Julie closed the door behind her. "That was weird."

Kristine was on the brink of tears. "I know." She crossed the rectangular-shaped room and sank miserably into a seat and put her head in her hands. "Where's Kelsey? And why hasn't he looked into Abby's disappearance?"

"And why did he say that Abby never came here?" Julie whispered as she bowed her head and crossed her arms over her chest. She was worried that if she spoke any louder that she would cry. She now could see that she had clearly been wrong; something bad really *was* going on, and Kristine had a right to worry.

Suddenly she heard Zach's voice in the back of her head saying the exact same thing that he'd said at the campout: *Whatever it is, it'll be okay.*

Then as if a hypnotist had snapped his fingers, Julie forgot that Abby and Kelsey had vanished into thin air. All the remorse left her body, and she couldn't remember why she was in the Dr. Culbreth's waiting room. She looked up and saw Kristine crying her eyes out, but Julie couldn't piece together any reason why she'd be crying. Julie decided that Kristine was really embarrassing herself by crying like this in front of someone else.

Kristine found some strength and raised her head out of her hands about an inch, long enough to see Julie walking away. *She doesn't even care!* thought Kristine. There was no combination of words to describe how furious she was at Julie. *It's bad enough that two girls could be lying somewhere cold, alone, and hurt, but to make it worse, all she cares about is herself,* Kristine assumed.

Suddenly a boy with medium-length, auburn hair walked in and took a seat next to her. "Are you okay?" he asked as he bent down a little so that he could see her face. His voice was filled with genuine concern.

"No. No, I'm not." Kristine sighed as she sat all the way up and slumped against the back of the chair.

"What's wrong?" he asked with a little curiosity in his eyes.

"Two of my friends are missing, and my roommate is acting like two completely different people. And one of the people she seems to act the most like is a snob." Kristine ran a hand through her hair in frustration. "I don't know what to do."

"How is she acting like a snob?"

"Well, at first, she was acting like the real her, who is a very nice, very good person. So we came down here to see if Dr. Culbreth had found one of our friends who went missing, and in the end, we ended up finding out that *another* one of our friends is missing, and we got kicked out of the dean's office. So I'm sitting here crying, and she teases me by acting like she actually cared, and then she just walks out on me and leaves me to cry my eyes out! Two girls are lying out there hurt, possibly dead, and she doesn't even care! I swear, when she acts like that, it's like all she thinks about is herself!" Kristine couldn't help it. Every second from the previous moment streamed out of her. It was like she had had a lid over her mouth and this person had removed it by simply asking her about Julie and now everything was pouring out. "I'm being rude. My name's Kristine."

"Garret." He smiled. "I heard about Abby's disappearance too. And if it helps, she was my friend also."

"You knew Abby? Then how come I never saw you around . . . back home I mean?" Kristine stuttered.

"We took karate together." A cloud slowly covered Garret's eyes, but it passed as quickly as it had come. "One thing I know for sure is she'll be okay. If I know Abby, and I do, she probably blew this Popsicle stand, and trust me, if anyone does try to hurt her, they will get their butts kicked."

"What makes you so sure?"

"Well, Salfira said that she probably escaped and that she'd be okay, and if she said it, then it must be true," Garret explained as if it was obvious. "Gotta go. I'm supposed to meet up with some of the guys so we can grab seats together at dinner." And as he spoke, he rose to leave.

Kristine had sat up straight when he said that he knew Abby. Now she watched him leave in confusion. "Who's Salfira?" she whispered to no one in particular. *When did these kids start to act so strange?* she asked herself. *When did Julie start acting so weird?* It didn't take her that long to realize it was after she drank the drink Zach gave her. *I knew he was no good*, she thought. She stood up and walked into the hallway. She quickly walked down to the grand hall. Anyone could see that she was angry and avoided her stare. She kept stopping and asking people if they'd seen Zach, and she was pointed in various directions until she finally found him in the grand hall. She stormed up to him and demanded to talk to him alone. His friends scattered, and she set her venomous gaze on Zach. "Listen, you jerk," Kristine spat. "I'm on to you."

"Huh?" Zach's face betrayed that he had no idea what she was talking about, but she could see his eyes taunting her.

Kristine scowled. "Stop playing dumb."

"I'm not playing. I honestly don't know what you're talking about." Zach's expression didn't change.

Kristine wanted to scream at him she was so mad. She somehow managed to stay calm. "I know you did something to Julie. I don't know if you put something in the drink you gave her at the campout or if it was something else, but I know you did it."

"Kristine, do you honestly think—"

She didn't let him finish. "I also know you know something about the disappearances of Abby Cooper and Kelsey Dickerson."

"Who?"

Kristine couldn't contain her rage any longer, and she let it bubble over to the surface. She stomped on Zach's foot as hard as she could, and she could have sworn she broke his foot.

She was about to walk away when Zach, while holding his throbbing foot with one hand, grabbed Kristine's elbow with the other. She spun around in shock, and to her disbelief, Zach whispered something she would never forget: "You can't save the missing girls. Neither can you save the girls we're yet to take."

Kristine stumbled back in fear. Suddenly the dinner buffet appeared, and through the sudden stampede of kids, Kristine could no longer see Zach.

"Kristine!" Julie called. Kristine spun around and saw Julie, Qwin, Lacy, TJ, and Morgan standing by the table. Julie's grinned quickly faded when she saw how pale her roommate was. Kristine couldn't help it; she bolted out of the grand hall and ran down the corridors. She didn't know where she was running; she just knew that she was. She ended up in her and Julie's room. She threw herself on her bed and began to cry.

Julie had been able to tell something was wrong with Kristine. She turned to Qwin, who stood in front of her in the buffet line and handed her the plate she been holding. "Get me some chicken tacos and hot sauce."

Qwin looked at her with confusion. "Where are you going?"

"Kristine was crying," Julie explained with concern as she quickly broke from the buffet line to follow her roommate before she lost her.

Julie tried to follow Kristine through the winding halls of the oppressive school, but Kristine had been running, and Julie had gotten a late start in following her, so she quickly lost her. Julie stood at the cross-section between two different hallways for a long time trying to decide if she should keep going and probably get lost or just talk to Kristine later that night; she went with talk to her later, then she turned around and went back to the grand hall.

CHAPTER SIX

That night in their dorm, Julie had gotten back from dinner early, and with her she'd brought a plate of food she'd saved for Kristine. Julie found her lying face down on her pillow, sobbing. Julie set the plate down on the floor by her roommate's bed and quickly sat down beside her. She gently placed her hand on her shoulder, "Kristine? Are you okay? What's wrong?"

Julie was the last person Kristine wanted to see; she was just a reminder of how powerless she was feeling. She mumbled into her pillow, "Leave me alone!" But the words came out muffled, and Julie didn't understand.

"Huh? I don't know if you're hungry, but you missed dinner, so I brought you some food."

Kristine couldn't take it anymore; she just wanted Julie to go away and quit making her think about how she was so helpless to save Abby or Kelsey. She shoved herself up from the pillow and turned to Julie, "I *said* leave me alone!"

Julie was taken aback by the sudden burst of anger. She cautiously rose from the bed and picked up the plate, offering it to Kristine, "Food?" She almost whispered, uncertain what Kristine would do.

Kristine scowled at the plate of chicken enchiladas. "I'm not hungry." And with that she buried her face in her pillow and resumed crying until she was out of tears.

The next day, Julie stood in the west garden with TJ. Ms. Lindsey had allowed the two kids time after school so that Julie could tutor TJ in broom flying. So far, Julie could see why TJ needed a tutor. He couldn't stay on his broom; plus, he had no control over it. The first time TJ lifted off the ground, his broom began to kick and fly around quickly and stop abruptly in a desperate attempt to get TJ off. Julie had observed that for someone who couldn't hang on to his broom, when his life was being threatened by one, he could hang on pretty well. And when his broom wasn't raging out of control, TJ couldn't hang on. It was like someone had smeared his fingers in butter! The longest he'd been able to hold on was five minutes. Julie now stood holding a stopwatch, quickly looking back and forth between TJ and his time. TJ was clinging to his broom for dear life; Julie had to give him props, though. This was the highest he'd managed to lift off the ground.

"You know you're the first wizard I've met who's afraid of heights." Julie sighed indifferently.

"This isn't as easy as it looks," TJ shot with a wavering voice.

"TJ, I can fly fifty miles an hour at three hundred feet," Julie returned. Some people thought Julie was exaggerating when she said this, but as it turned out, she really could fly that high and that fast and be in complete control of her broom while doing it.

"Showoff," TJ mumbled.

"Hey, there's some good news," Julie revealed.

"What?"

"You're breaking your personal height record."

"Really?" TJ smiled. "What height?"

"An inch and a half. Which is half an inch more than you had when we started," Julie explained.

"How long have I been on my broom?" TJ whined.

"In fifteen seconds, you'll have been on for minute," Julie read off the stopwatch. "You know you can do better than this, TJ."

TJ managed to get his broom down to the ground. He dismounted and tossed his broom in the grass. "I know."

"So why don't you?"

"How am I supposed to know?" TJ snapped.

"That's a good reason," Julie nodded. "You remember my brother, Nathan?"

"What does he have to do with anything?" TJ shrugged.

"When my dad was teaching Nathan how to fly, he had this trick to help Nathan hold on to his broom that always worked," Julie explained.

TJ looked at her suspiciously. "What was it?"

Julie held one hand palm up as if she was showing him something, and with a flick of her wrist, a role of duct tape appeared in her hands. There were some spells that Julie had done so many times in her lifetime, and her mind was so used to doing that it got the point where she didn't even need to recite certain spells anymore. She could just run them through her mind, and they happened.

"You're going to duct tape my mouth shut? How's that gonna help?"

"I'm going to tape your hands to your broom." Julie sighed as if it had been obvious.

"Are you sure that's safe?" TJ stared suspiciously at the duct tape. He wasn't a fan of the idea. What if he needed to get off his boom straightaway? "Didn't Nathan get hit by a flying carpet all because his hands were duct-taped to his broom and he couldn't dismount?"

"Yeah, but he lived. And plus, after his accident, he never fell off his broom again." Julie walked over to where TJ had tossed his broom in the grass and was about to pick it up when a confused look crossed her face. "Isn't this where you threw your broom in the grass?"

"Yeah," TJ muttered as he turned and walked to her side.

"Well, it isn't there anymore," Julie countered.

"What?" TJ would be in huge trouble if his parents heard that his broom went missing. "It has to be there. This is exactly where I threw it!"

"No need to panic yet," Julie soothed. "Maybe we're just looking in the wrong place. Look around and see if you can find it."

The two searched for half an hour with no luck. Finally they collapsed in the middle of the field. TJ scowled. "Maybe if they actually mowed the west garden instead of letting the grass and weeds grow knee high, then maybe when student wizards threw their brooms down they could actually find them!"

Suddenly something connected in Julie's head, and her face grew red with anger. She turned to TJ; it took all her strength not to yell at him. "You *threw* your broom in the grass? Throw as in *tossing* it there and *walking away?*"

"Yeah, why?"

"Here's something I learned from experience." Julie couldn't hold it in anymore. This was the first thing they taught you in Ms. Lindsey's class, and he wasn't even listening when she said it! Even Julie had known this before she came to this stupid school. "You are supposed to *set* your broom down over by the magnets by the shed!" Julie gestured to the old tin shed at the front of the field by the school. "The magnets connect with the magnets in the top of the brooms and keep the brooms from *running away!* When you don't, disloyal brooms like yours will sneak away!"

"So my broom ran away?"

"Yes!"

"My dad is going to kill me!" TJ fretted as he put his head in his hands and began to shake it in dismay.

I know I'm going to regret this, Julie thought. She stood up and offered TJ a hand. He took it, and as soon as he was up, Julie grabbed his wrist and started dragging him in the direction of the shed. "Where are we going?" TJ questioned.

"You can practice on my broom," Julie offered. Suddenly Julie turned in the direction of the west tower entrance. She stood perfectly still, and she looked concerned as she stared at the empty door. TJ turned and abruptly saw what Julie was looking at. Zach Forrests was walking toward them from the west tower. Well, he wasn't really walking. You could see he was on a pair of crutches and had a brace on one of his feet. Julie began to walk toward him, dragging TJ behind her. Zach, Julie, and TJ met halfway there. TJ pulled his arm from Julie's grasp and rubbed where she'd squeezed it.

"What happened?" Julie demanded.

"Well, your friend Kristine smashed my foot." He sent Julie a smile to assure that there were no hard feelings between them.

"What? How?" Julie fretted.

"I was in the grand hall waiting for the dinner table, and she just walked up to me and stomped on my foot with all her strength. And when I asked her why, she said it was because she was bored," Zach said, but TJ saw Zach's left eye twitch.

"Remind me to congratulate Kristine," TJ shot.

Zach ignored his comment. "Now I can't compete in the broom races."

"Broom races?" Julie wondered.

Oh, no, TJ thought. *I know that look in her eyes.*

"Oh, yeah," Zach continued. "The school is holding its annual broom racing competition in a few weeks. You know, I hear they have this awesome obstacle course and everything. I'm surprised you didn't know. The whole school is talking about it! The signup sheets and info packets are in the dean's waiting room. Now that you know, are you going to be in the race?"

"Julie, can I talk to you alone?" TJ pleaded.

"This will only take a minute," Julie promised Zach. TJ dragged Julie about thirty feet away and then turned to face her.

"He lied about how Kristine broke his foot—if she even broke his foot at all. I don't think we should trust this guy," TJ begged.

"TJ, you're just saying that because you don't like this guy. You know, he said you might do something like this because you were jealous of how much attention I'm giving him," Julie snapped.

"What? Julie, that's not true! I know he was lying to us!" TJ cried.

"Oh, really, TJ?" Julie was chagrined. She didn't want to hear this.

"His left eye twitched when he was talking about Kristine! When people are lying about something, their eyes either go to the left or the right or one eye twitches. It's a known fact." TJ was sure she'd believe him now he had credible evidence.

Julie, jaw set, arms crossed tightly over her chest, turned and started to walk in the direction of the west tower.

"Where are you going?" TJ called after her.

"Back to the real world!" Julie shouted over her shoulder. "Maybe you should come with me and leave all your backward lies!"

TJ didn't see another choice other than following Julie back to the west tower; after all, that was the only way out of the west garden. Zach had been sitting patiently in the grass waiting for them. When they got close, he stood up and smiled. "So are you going to be in the race?"

Julie turned and saw TJ standing behind her with a pleading look on his face. She turned back to Zach. "I'd love to."

TJ followed the two up the winding staircase that led from the west garden into the school. They passed the hallway that led into the west tower and kept going up. Soon the stairs gave way to Window Lane, and the three kept going toward the wing of the school to Dr. Culbreth's waiting room. Julie and Zach walked ahead and talked while TJ trudged behind in silence. Finally they reached the waiting room and saw the sign-up sheets pinned up to the opposite wall and a stack of info packs on the receptionist's desk. Julie was about to sign up as Zach sat down in one of the chairs, and TJ grabbed Julie's arm. She turned to face TJ. "This better not be about Zach."

"Fine," TJ grumbled. "But don't say I never warned you."

"Can I say you never warned me about *rational* things?" Julie shot.

TJ watched her in aggravation as she walked over to the sign-up sheet and put down her name and dorm number. TJ suddenly had an idea that would show Julie, but it might also kill him. He couldn't believe he was about to do this. After Julie had gone to get an info sheet, TJ went over and signed himself up for the broom race.

Julie spun around in shock, and Zach stood up on his crutches. "What do you think you're doing?" Julie cried in exasperation.

"TJ, you can't fly!" Zach proclaimed as he hopped to his side. "Can he?" Zach asked Julie in confusion.

"No, he can't. He can barely get an inch and a half off the ground, plus his broom ran away today," Julie disclosed.

"The info packet says the race isn't until February. That's plenty of time for me to practice," TJ insisted. "I'll be good at flying by then."

"There's not enough time in the world," Zach muttered.

"You still don't have a broom," Julie protested.

"There has to be a spell or something that can bring it back," TJ suggested.

"There are spell books in the library. We might be able to find something to get your broom back," Julie realized.

"Do you want him to die?" Zach questioned.

"Look at it this way," Julie explained. "Either he kills himself in this race, or his dad will kill him for losing the broom in the first place, so we might as well help him."

"Whatever. I have to go," Zach mumbled as he hopped to the door.

"Where're you going?" TJ called.

"I have a checkup with the nurse about my foot," he grumbled.

Julie sighed. "Come on, TJ. We're going to the library." TJ and Julie walked into the deserted hallway. Julie stood still for a long time looking both ways until finally she whispered, "TJ?"

"Yeah?" he answered from behind her.

"Where's the library?"

TJ didn't know why he'd thought that Julie knew where the library was; after all, she only read books when it was a matter of life and death, which, with her clumsy spell casting, was often. Then again, TJ didn't know where the school's library was either. He'd had no need to go there since their arrival. He felt embarrassed and sighed. "I don't know."

"So what do we do?" Julie stammered.

"Ask Dr. Culbreth?" TJ guessed.

"Aww, but he hates me," Julie whined. Then something about Dr. Culbreth reminded her about her missing friends, and she suddenly felt extremely sad. "TJ?"

She didn't realize he'd been talking as she'd been thinking, "Well you know that's too bad, because I don't see any other way we're going to find—" He realized he should stop before she turned around and went back to her dorm.

"What?" TJ was sure that she was going to say something, such as that he'd better shut up if he wanted her help, so he was already preparing himself to walk off after finding out where the library was and leave her here by herself, but what she did say came as a shock to him.

Julie whispered, "Kelsey and Abby are missing."

TJ frowned. He was suddenly worried about his friend's mental health. "Julie," he started. "They've been missing for days, and you knew that too. You and Kristine were the first ones to find out."

Julie's head was spinning. "Go ask Dr. Culbreth where the library is. I need to sit down."

TJ nodded. "Okay, but are you sure you'll be okay out here by yourself?"

"Yeah, just go ask about the library. I'll be right here when you get back," Julie assured him. But she knew that TJ wasn't concerned about whether or not she'd leave him; it was whether or not her head was all right. She watched TJ enter the office anyway. Julie suddenly felt a voice in her head trying to make her forget about Abby and Kelsey. Julie pushed against it so hard that her head began to throb; it was a fight Julie couldn't win. And just like that, Abby and Kelsey were erased from Julie's mind for a second time. TJ walked out of the office and saw Julie waiting for him, looking as if the incident where Abby and Kelsey suddenly coming to her mind had never happened.

"You okay?" TJ slowly questioned.

"Sure, I guess," Julie answered unsurely. "Do you know where the library is?"

"Yeah, come on." And with that, the two kids walked down the hall. When they came to an intersection, TJ led them to the right. And after more turns and upward staircases that Julie could count, they reached a giant room filled with bookshelves, and every shelf was filled with books. Some were new, and some could have been used in the 1500s. They spotted the librarian's desk against the front wall and the librarian reading *Wizards Weekly*, a very popular magazine in the magic world.

The two kids walked up to the dusty, musky-smelling desk. When the librarian didn't move, TJ cleared his throat. The librarian refused to acknowledge the children's existence. Julie looked down at the nameplate on the desk, but all it said was "Librarian." While TJ cleared his throat again, Julie noticed a service bell on the desk next to the nameplate. Julie rang the bell, and finally the librarian put her magazine down, and all three of them cried out in surprise.

"What are *you* doing here?" Mrs. Sawyer hissed from behind the desk.

"Us? What are you doing here?" Julie screamed.

"And where's the librarian?" TJ panicked.

"I am the librarian," Mrs. Sawyer barked. "What are you doing here, Julian? I thought you didn't read?"

"I…I don't," Julie managed. "But TJ does."

An aggravated look crossed the librarian's face as she turned to TJ. It was clear she didn't like either student, or maybe she hated all students in general. "What are you looking for?" She seethed.

"Where are the spell books?" TJ wondered.

"Those are for teachers only." Mrs. Sawyer seemed satisfied that she got to disappoint them. "Now *get out!*"

The two kids ran out of the room faster than a cheetah. As they walked through the halls on their way to their dorms, TJ was disappointed, and Julie was forming a plan in her head. TJ complained, "Now my dad will murder me."

"Don't be so sure." Julie smiled mischievously.

"What are you thinking?" TJ questioned nervously. Julie's plans always worked, but afterward, 50 percent of the time TJ would end up taking the rap if they got caught for what Julie did.

"Do you remember how I got detention?" Julie began.

"Yeah, you were caught outside of your dorm on our day off. You also turned Mrs. Sawyer into a big chicken," TJ recalled.

"Well, before I gave Mrs. Sawyer feathers, I visited Mr. Sawyer's classroom." Julie watched TJ's mouth fall open, and he stopped walking. She quickly grabbed his arm and pulled him along. "Come on, TJ. Who knows how many secret passages there are in the school? Someone could be listening to us right now!"

TJ quickened his pace as he and Julie hurried toward their dorms. In a low whisper, TJ scolded, "What were you doing there?"

"I was looking through his potion recipes," she explained. "You know, in case I ever wanted to have some fun in detention. But I heard him starting to come down the stairs, so I ripped a page out of his recipes book and hid in between two tables. Whenever he went to his ingredients cabinet and turned around to examine his ingredients, I ran. Later that night, when Kristine was asleep, I took the page out and looked at it under a flashlight to see what I took."

"You mean you took it without looking? What if it was something really important that he will notice was gone?" TJ worried. "Julie," he began in a much calmer tone, "what did you take?"

"Don't worry. I'm sure it wasn't important, but it *can* help us get a spell book," Julie assured.

"Julie, what did you take?" TJ pleaded.

"I took the recipe for an invisibility potion," Julie uncovered.

TJ stopped, his face pale. "Julie, that is very important. And if you stole it from a potion recipe book, the owner is sure as heck is going to notice!"

"This is bad, isn't it?" Julie asked as she turned to face TJ.

"This is very bad!" TJ raised his voice.

Julie suddenly felt sick. "Oh, what are we going to do?"

"We?" TJ cried. "Last time I checked, this was your mess. You got yourself into this. You have to get yourself out. Have fun." TJ started to walk away.

Julie knew she need TJ's help to replace what she took, and she also knew TJ needed her help to get his broom back. *Hey,* Julie thought, *that adds up!* "Good luck explaining to your dad how you lost your broom!" she called after him. TJ stopped and turned to face her. "Face it, TJ." Julie smiled. "You need me, and I need you. Everything is falling into place."

"Fine," TJ gave in. "Let's head back to my dorm. You can tell me the plan there."

The two reached the dorm an hour before the boys' meeting. TJ hoped that her plan wasn't so complicated that it would take longer than half an hour; he still had business to take care of that Julie wasn't supposed to know about. Morgan was suspicious about TJ bringing someone that was considered an enemy to their dorm, but TJ assured him that he only had the best of intentions.

"So here's my plan," Julie began. "Later on tonight I'll sneak into the east garden and steal the required ingredients—"

Morgan interrupted, "When tonight?"

"About midnight probably," Julie estimated.

"How do you know the way into the east garden?" TJ demanded.

"Zach showed me a secret passage in Window Lane." Julie smiled as if it was one of the greatest things that had ever happened to her.

A wave of worry and sadness swept over him. Kelsey and Abby had walked into the east garden the day before they vanished. Now Julie was going to disappear too. Despite her status in his head as an evil genius and how she had tricked him into helping her replace a serious theft, deep, deep, deep down, she was a good person and a great friend.

"TJ, don't look so disappointed in me." Julie frowned. "I didn't actually go in the east garden. We barely made it halfway down the steps before we heard people coming and had to come up and hide the entrance."

TJ smiled. She was safe—for now. He realized he had been disappointed, but not for the reason Julie thought. He'd thought he'd lost her. His thoughts were interrupted by Julie continuing her plan to get him a spell book.

"I'll take the ingredients back to my room and turn them into a potion. The recipe says it has to sit for forty-eight hours, so when time's up, TJ can drink it, get a book from the library, and be back here before anyone else is awake," Julie finished, quite proud of herself.

"What about the spell for my broom?" TJ questioned.

"We'll look for the spell the night after that. Any other problems?"

"One more thing." TJ sighed. "If we're actually going through with this, spit shake you're going to take all the rap for this," TJ ordered, holding out his hand.

"I may not be book smart like you, but I am street smart. And one thing I know from being street smart is that taking that deal assures my expulsion, and if I end up leaving this school that way, my dad will send me to military school," Julie explained her logic.

"And I won't get expelled if *I'm* caught?" TJ cried.

"Of course not. Dr. Culbreth loves you," Julie lied.

"Why?" TJ asked, unsure he wanted to hear the answer.

"Because you haven't been sent to his office yet." Julie and Morgan sighed as if it were obvious.

TJ looked at Morgan for verification. "It's true." Morgan nodded. "He finds kids who haven't been sent to his office yet a breath of fresh air."

"Mainly because almost every kid has been sent to his office," Julie dragged on.

"And plus it's not every day he sees a kid in his office without a criminal record," Morgan added.

"Fine," TJ agreed. "I'll do it." TJ glanced at his watch. He only had half an hour before the meeting.

"So how are you going to solve my problem?" Julie wondered.

"Duplicate the recipe and replace the original before Mr. Sawyer knows it's missing," TJ said in one breath. "Now get back to your dorm before someone sees you." Julie got up and walked out the door. TJ turned to Morgan. "I have to go invite someone to tonight's meeting."

CHAPTER SEVEN

Kristine was sitting on her bed doing her history homework when someone poofed into her room. She assumed that it was Julie and didn't bother to look up. She heard the person who she assumed was Julie walk across the room to Kristine's bed, and then they tapped on her shoulder. *What does that witch with a capital B want now?* Kristine thought to herself. The person tapped on her shoulder again. "What do you want?" spat Kristine.

"I heard you broke Zach's foot." TJ smiled at the idea. Why hadn't he thought about that?

Kristine looked up from her homework and took her iPod headphones out of her ears. Her parents had bought her an iPod for Christmas so she'd have a way to listen to music when she was in public, around mortals, and she had taken quite a liking to the idea of music coming out of a box that no one else could hear. No wizard had invented a magical object like that before, so Kristine and just about every other magical being who'd ever tried listening to an iPod actually kept one for when they were board. "Oh, sorry, TJ. Thought you were Julie. Where is she?" Kristine realized for the first time how late it was. An alarmed look crossed her face. "You don't think she's been 'called home by her parents'?"

"No, she's on her way back here. I saw her a few minutes ago," TJ said in one breath.

Kristine sighed. "Good. I may not like her that much now, but that doesn't mean she wasn't a good friend at some point. So what are you doing here, TJ?"

"Did you really break Zach's foot?" TJ questioned.

"Yeah, you should have seen his face!" Kristine laughed.

The two kids high-fived. TJ was grinning from ear to ear. "Look, some of the guys and I have been having secret meetings after curfew to try and figure out why some of the girls were acting so strange. All we know is that we should keep an eye on Zach and that the girls started acting weird the night of the campout." As TJ began, he became more and more serious.

"And you're here because you think I might know something?" Kristine guessed the ending.

"Which is why I'm inviting you to our meeting tonight," TJ added. "Plus, you're pretty much the only girl we can trust right now. Morgan and I both agreed on that. So will you come?"

"Sure," Kristine agreed as she climbed off the bed. "By the way, I know a lot."

"Good." TJ sighed. "Because we scarcely know anything. This room is way too warm. Take us to me and Morgan's dorm!" In a flash of light, the two showed up in the boys' dorm. Kristine sat down on the bed closest to the door and turned to face the two boys who sat across from her. The door opened, and the trio turned to face the newcomer.

Conner stood open-mouthed in the doorway when he saw Kristine in the room. He stared at her for a moment and then turned his gaze to the two guys sitting on the other bed. "What the heck?" he asked.

"She's the only girl we can trust," Morgan said. "Now get in here before someone sees you!"

Conner stepped into the room and closed the door behind him. He still sent Kristine cautious glares. "How do we know we can trust her?"

"Dude, she hasn't started acting strange. She's been doing some research of her own, and we need the info she has, and plus, she broke the suspect's foot," TJ defended.

"Fine," Conner grumbled. "But don't think the other guys are going to be as cool as me."

The other guys weren't, but TJ and Morgan managed to convince them to stay. They all sat where they had the previous meeting, and Kristine sat on the bed that all the boys had their backs up against. TJ stood in front of the white board where everything from the last meeting was still up there. He began the meeting. "I know some of you aren't so sure about Morgan and I adding Kristine in the meetings, but you'll be singing a different tune when you hear what she has to say. Kristine, you may take the stage."

She solemnly stood, and she began when she knew she had all the boys' attention.

Julie skulked through the hallway as quietly as she could. She looked down at the blueprints she'd stolen from Mr. Sawyer's room when she'd taken the potion recipe. The weird thing was the papers had been torn out of the same book. Julie had known this when she looked at the papers under the flashlight that night in her and Kristine's room. Julie had also figured out that she had not stolen from a potions book; she didn't know what she had stolen from. Therefore, she couldn't duplicate the papers. She had chosen not to tell TJ this part of her story because he had a tendency to overreact.

Even though she was trying to be quiet, she couldn't help but mutter to herself, "The worst situations seem to just find me, don't they? I steal from a book that I think is a potion book, and it turns out to be something else after it's too late. And not only do I steal a recipe, no. Stupid old me had to steal the blueprints for this dumb place!"

Julie tried to match where she was to one of the passages on the blueprints; she'd never been any good at reading these things. She matched the turn up ahead to a turn at the end of the end hallway on the old map that she suspected she was in. Sure, she could have just used the map she was given when she first signed in, but she had lost it already. As soon as they were done, he'd make her destroy the blueprints. She looked at the prints and saw that she had three more turns to make after this, and then she'd reach Window Lane, or at least, she hoped she would. Suddenly her thoughts were interrupted by the sounds of footsteps around the corner.

"For those of you who don't know," Kristine began as she stood, head high despite the angry glares that fell upon her, "Kelsey's missing."

Adam's mouth fell open, and he scrambled to his feet. "That's impossible! I only saw her a few days ago!"

"Like Abby," Kristine continued sympathetically, "Kelsey vanished the day after she was seen walking in the east garden. I'm really sorry, Adam." She turned sympathetically to Adam, who looked devastated. "She was my friend too."

"Adam, would you like to take a night off and maybe go back to your room and get some sleep?" Morgan politely suggested. "Because, to be honest, you look a little green."

His face turned from green to beet red. "I'm not going anywhere! These guys have crossed a line! I'm not going to sleep until I know Kelsey's safe!"

TJ's eyes narrowed. "Depriving yourself of sleep won't help Kelsey."

Adam was adamant. "I'm still not leaving."

"Suit yourself." Kristine nodded then continued telling what she knew. "I agree with you guys that everything ties back to Zach Forrests, and for those of you who still don't trust me, I think it might comfort you a little if you know that I broke Zach's foot on purpose."

"I trust her," Max announced.

There were a few nods, and Max also earned two scowls. Kristine kept going anyway. "I have a theory. I think that Zach put something in Julie's drink and probably the other girls' too."

"But he was hanging out with Julie at the campfire. You sat with us. You know that." TJ narrowed his eyes skeptically.

"He sat with us at the *beginning* of dinner. I recall he spent the entire dining portion of the campout getting Julie a refill on her punch when it doesn't take that long to walk over to the refreshment table and get more punch," Kristine defended. "And multiple people say that all the girls listed on the white board here"—Kristine turned and gestured to the white board behind her—"were given refills by Zach."

"That's impossible," Conner accused. "We were with our girlfriends all night."

"Were you with them every minute?"

The boys glanced at each other guiltily. "Well, no."

Ms. Edwards and Ms. Lindsey walked down the corridor nonchalantly on their way back to their rooms. "He's looked everywhere!" Ms. Lindsey whispered. "The recipe and the map are gone! They were just torn out of the book! What if a student found them?"

Just before the two rounded the bend, Ms. Edwards grabbed her shoulder, and the two stopped walking. "For Pete's sake,

Rena! The pages went missing on an off day! There were no kids outside of the housing wings. Well, there was one student who was found outside her dorm, but she was in the east tower."

Ms. Lindsey sighed, and the two started walking again. "Julian Lynnel walked across campus from her dorm through the school wing just to pull a prank that she knew might get her expelled. Why wouldn't she stop by a classroom to see if there was anything interesting that she wanted to steal?" The two rounded the corner into the next hallway. "It was Julian Lynnel. I just know it."

"Know what?" The two professors looked up to see that they had almost walked into Dr. Culbreth.

"Hello, sir," the two teachers greeted.

"Hello." He frowned. "Now, what is it that you are so certain you know?"

"She believes that Julian Lynnel stole the missing pages," Ms. Edwards informed.

"Julian Lynnel! I should have known!" Their boss growled. "I will look into this at once!"

"As you should." Ms. Lindsey nodded.

"I do believe I'm in a bit of a hurry though, ladies." Dr. Culbreth rushed off. "So I'm afraid I'll have to go now."

Dr. Culbreth rounded the bend, and as soon as the teachers were out of sight, he pressed his back against the wall. "Lies, lies, lies. I don't need a disguise!" With a flash of white light, the person the teachers *thought* was Dr. Culbreth transformed back into herself—Julie Lynnel. "I hate doing that," she whined. "It hurts so badly when your skeletal system morphs so that you look like someone else."

Back in Amarillo, Julie was known for an extremely short attention span and slacking off. This was one of those times where the size of her attention span kicked in. Julie suddenly started letting her mind wander from the tasks at hand as she raced down the rest of the corridors.

"I know Zach is connected with the disappearances of Abby and Kelsey," Kristine added. The boys' guilt was suddenly replaced by shock. This was a serious accusation; she needed proof, though, to be proved correct.

"Kristine," TJ asked seriously, "do you have proof?"

"Before I broke Zach's foot, I was accusing him of basically everything you guys suspect. But he just kept taunting me and saying he didn't do it, so I broke his foot, and when I started to walk away, he grabbed my arm and told me, and I quote, 'You can't save the missing girls. Neither can you save ones we're yet to take,'" Kristine finished miserably.

"Thank you, Kristine." TJ clapped as he stood up and patted Kristine on the back. She took a seat on the bed, and TJ took his place in front of the white board. "Does anyone else have any knew info?"

"I think I might have something," Garret admitted, standing up.

"Go ahead." TJ stepped aside to let Garret take the stage.

"Does anyone know or heard of a Salfira? Last name unknown," Garret questioned. His only answer was confused looks and shaking heads. "I ran into a girl named Salfira on the way back to my dorm after the last meeting. She spilled what she said was ice water on my front. She said that she had gotten it from the kitchen, and that was the only reason she was up. Then I ran into Mr. Sawyer, who said that he had a full bottle of belief charm stolen from his stash only an hour before I showed up. He also said that the school didn't have a kitchen."

"We don't have anyone else's word on her yet, so we can't say that this girl is a suspect—" TJ started to say.

"I wasn't suggesting she had anything to do with it," Garret interrupted.

"So what were you suggesting?" Hudson asked.

Julie finally raced into Window Lane. She doubled over on her hands and knees gasping for breath in the middle of the lane. As soon she had enough air, she stood up straight and looked both ways. When she was sure that there was no one coming, she stomped on one part of the floor then another. After a few stomps, she heard a hollow sound. Julie got down on her hands and knees in the middle of the lane and started brushing dirt away from the ground until she found the latch. She brushed some more dirt away and found the spell lock. A spell lock was like a pad lock, but they weren't opened by keys; they were opened by specific lock and unlock spells that only the owner knew.

Julie knew the unlock spell because when Zach had brought her here for the first time, he had whispered the spell, so Julie had heard it and memorized it. She reached out her hand and placed it over a small section of the filthy, dirt covered floor. "Open up, let me in. Show me the secret you hold within." With a high-pitched mix of a squeak and a clink, the trapped door pop opened an inch. Julie lifted it the rest of the way; it squeaked so loudly in the process she had to look both ways again just to make sure no one was coming. Then, when she was sure she hadn't woken up anyone, she raced down the stairs that the trap door had revealed.

She finally reached the end of the stairs or, as Zach called it, "the dead end." He called it that because it looked like a solid wall of cement brick, but Julie knew better. She placed her hand sideways at the top of the wall. A white light ran down the wall slowly as she quickly casted, "Solid brick, dissolve quick!" Then she removed her hand and took a step back. She was about to walk through the wall when she heard the trap door slam shut, and she heard the loud click of the spell lock being locked. Julie suddenly realized she wasn't alone in the passage and quickly stepped through the wall. The east garden opened up before her. She stepped out of the invisible passage entry and hugged the wall of the school so no one in Window Lane would see her.

After a long moment of silence, Julie slowly began to walk down the cobblestone path through the first part of the garden. To the unknowing eye, it looked like a rose garden, but Julie knew better. Every flower was unknown to the mortal world, and they were all ingredients to multiple potions, but they weren't dangerous. It was the plants in the center of the huge garden that were poisonous if used in the wrong way. Julie needed some of those plants to create the invisibility potion. Julie took her canvas bag off her shoulder and started looking at some of the nonpoisonous flowers; she needed three of these. She just hoped that she would pick the right ones. She quickly turned around and looked up at the windows of Window Lane. She didn't see anyone—yet. She couldn't help but wonder, though, who had entered the passage after her. A spell lock could only be unlocked from one side, and that meant...*Oh, no.* Julie gasped. She was stuck in a restricted area of the school.

"I was suggesting," Garret quietly defended, "that she was hot."

Everyone else looked at each other and then back at Garret. "You're my friend, Garret." TJ sighed as he stood up and put his hand on his back and began to lead him to the door. "But I'm gonna have to ask you not to come back to these meetings anymore." Garret tried to object, but TJ slammed the door in his face. He turned back to the group of kids. "We can't trust anything he says."

"But we will have to watch out for a Salfira," Max pointed out.

"Is that all?" Houston whined. "Because that took ten minutes to learn something that takes three seconds to say."

"It's not his fault." TJ sighed from his place on his bed. "He was intoxicated."

Every head turned. "What?"

"He smelled like belief charm. This Salfira, we need to know something more about her by the next meeting. Until then"—TJ stood and crossed the room to the door and opened it—"meeting adjourned." Everyone walked out the door. Before Kristine could leave, TJ grabbed her arm, and she stopped to look at him. "Not you."

"What?" Kristine asked as she turned to face him.

"You and I have to go make sure someone isn't getting herself killed," TJ explained.

TJ and Kristine waited until the hallway was clear and then started toward Window Lane. "How could you be so irresponsible?" Kristine whispered angrily.

TJ told her the whole story while they had waited, and Kristine had been furious that TJ had let Julie go out on her own when she was probably the next to go missing. "Julie's been my friend since kindergarten. Don't let our current arguments fool you. But the point is I know her, and she doesn't need us watching her every move."

"Then why do *you* want to go after her?" Kristine shot as she quickened her pace.

"Because she's been gone longer than she should have been," TJ answered.

Suddenly they saw another student coming toward them with a canvas bag on her shoulder. Once they got closer, they recognized Qwin, who was almost jogging toward them in a hurry. "She...she...Julie." Qwin gasped for breath.

Kristine took Qwin's shoulders and looked her in the eyes. "Take a deep breath, Qwin. Now, what happened to Julie?"

"I was sneaking around the school like I always do at night, when I reached Window Lane. I was looking out the windows when I saw Julie in the east garden. She was all alone, and she looked frantic! I talked to her on her cell phone, since she always has it with her, and she said that the teachers put an enchantment on the garden and she couldn't poof out of there. But she could poof her bag up into the lane. She told me that she was going to poof it up, and it was really important that I find TJ and give it to him. I don't know why this bag was so important, but she said as soon as you get it go to your dorm and hide it—hide it well." By now Qwin had her breath and had explained her whole her story.

"But it's nearly sunrise. If we hide this, then we won't have time to come back and save her from being seen," Kristine objected. She let go of Qwin's shoulders.

"She said you might say that, and she wanted you to go on and stay in your dorms. And she also said, and I quote, 'If they see you, you will be in more trouble than I could ever imagine, which is why I won't let you come out here. I'm used to getting in trouble. It's just another lecture and more detention, so don't worry about me.'" Suddenly the golden rays from the sunrise began to pour through the hall from a small window farther down. "Kids will be waking up soon. We should go," Qwin suggested.

With that, the trio unwillingly turned and headed back to their rooms.

CHAPTER EIGHT

Julie sat in the dean's office, which in her opinion was extremely overcrowded. All the teachers were in the office with Dr. Culbreth staring at her menacingly. All the teachers were yelling at her so loudly that her ears were going to explode if they didn't stop, which was her only concern at the moment. Finally they stopped, and Dr. Culbreth sighed. "Young lady, what are we going to do with you?"

"Watch me run away while you angrily shake your fist, yelling, 'Rotten kid!'?" Julie answered. The people in the room only scowled at her. "That question was rhetorical, wasn't it?"

"I've got an idea," Mrs. Sawyer spoke up. "Why don't we suspend her powers and lock her alone in the detention room for a few days without food?"

"No!" Julie cried. But all the teachers were already agreeing, and Julie didn't like the smile that was spreading across Dr. Culbreth's face.

"It's unanimous!" Dr. Culbreth announced. He reached under his desk and pulled out a crystal ball, and all the teachers put their hands on top. When they began to chant something Julie didn't understand, a small ball of purple light appeared in the crystal ball and began to expand. Julie, in horror, realized what was going on. She raced to the door and tried to open it, but it was locked. She began to pound and kick and yell for help, but it was no use; no one would hear her in time. By that time, the light had engulfed the crystal ball and was beginning to spread outward toward Julie. The light engulfed Julie too, and Julie suddenly collapsed on the floor in pain. No matter how hard Julie pushed, the light wouldn't go away, and the pain grew and grew until Julie was curled up in a ball on the floor. Finally the light and the pain vanished all at once, and a blue light the size of a bowling ball was left in the crystal ball. Every few seconds lightning shot at the walls of the crystal ball but never passed through.

Julie was so frightened as she stood up, eyes locked on the crystal ball, that she didn't have the strength to finish the first sentence that came out of her mouth. "Is that..."

"Your powers?" Dr. Culbreth finished. "Yes, and they are suspended until further notice. Ms. Lindsey, kindly show Miss Lynnel to the detention room where she will stay for three days."

Kristine had finally found a good use for the magic mirror her grandmother had given her for her birthday. She had used it to call TJ; he was sitting impatiently in his bathroom in front of the mirror so Kristine could see him. She was sitting on her bed looking into the small mirror that could have been mistaken for a palm mirror a mortal would use to apply make-up. School was being postponed so that the teachers and dean could decide what to do with Julie. Kristine had taken the ingredients her room-mate had taken from the east garden, and they were currently under Julie's bed. To Kristine and TJ's shock, Julie had not only enclosed the potion recipe in the canvas bag but also blueprints of the school from back when it was first being built. "Do you think she went to return the recipe to the book but didn't have enough time and accidentally stole the prints too?"

"No, Julie's stupid, but she's not that stupid," TJ explained.

"She still isn't back from the office yet," Kristine disclosed. "This can't be good."

Kristine was about to say something, but a loud voice poured through the halls, saying, "Classes will now continue. Please return to your homerooms."

Kristine was becoming ill with worry that another girl might be missing, and she kept telling herself over and over that she wasn't worried just because this girl was Julie.

"I'll see you in class?" TJ nervously questioned.

"Yes, and let's hope we see Julie there too." Kristine ended the connection between the two mirrors and slipped her own mirror into the pocket of her skirt. She stepped out of her dorm, but before she started toward class, she looked back at the portrait of the vampire slayer, and for a minute she thought she heard him *talk!*

"Pictures don't talk," she told herself. Kristine quickly looked away from the painting and started walking again when she heard it again, except this time she could distinctly hear the portrait talking. She moved slowly and cautiously toward the canvas painting until she was right next to it. She moved her ear closer to the painting so if it *was* talking she'd hear well.

"Help ..." Kristine jumped back in shock when she heard the ghostly whisper.

Her common sense told her to run and tell a teacher, but she was somehow rooted to the spot where she stood as if she couldn't move. While she was there, she heard the voice again, except this time the voice was louder, and Kristine knew just who it was.

"Help me, please! Kristine? TJ? Anyone?" Julie's voice pleaded.

Kristine stood up straight, angered by how stupid she'd been to fall for Julie's trick. *She's trying to scare me because I let her leave herself alone in the east garden!* "Julie, if you think I'm falling for your stupid trick, then you are dead wrong! Now come out from wherever you're hiding so I can go to class," Kristine demanded. But Julie didn't appear.

"Kristine?" Julie's voice rejoiced. "Where are you? Keep talking so that I can find you!"

"I'm serious!" Kristine yelled. "You have thirty seconds to come out, or I'm leaving without you!"

"I wish I knew how to come out," Julie's voice sounded pained. "They took my powers and locked me in the detention room, and now I'm wandering hopelessly through the tunnels looking for a way out!"

"How stupid do you think I am?" Kristine shouted. "Do I look like I was born yesterday? Don't answer that. Why can't you ever be serious about stuff, and why do you always have to be so annoying? You know what? I wish you were never born!"

Julie listened to Kristine's steps growing farther and farther away from the painting. Julie had been telling the truth and only wanted Kristine to help her out of the tunnels that led from the detention room. Julie sank into the corner she'd been standing in and wiped the tears from her face. Suddenly, again Abby and Kelsey came to her mind, and Julie kept trying to be brave, but the tears kept coming. She wondered where they were right now. *They're probably in a much better place than this,* Julie assumed. She wouldn't realize for much later that they were not.

TJ had already made it to what seemed like the center of a maze, but he knew it was the center of the school. It was the same circle of hallways that Garret had been dragged through the night he met Salfira. As TJ crossed to the hallway that led to the classroom, he looked up at the ceiling of the intersection. Rails stood at the end of the second- and third-floor halls that ended at the intersection. If he looked straight up, he'd see the school mural painted on the dome-shaped ceiling.

TJ had found the mural creepy since the day he first saw it. First of all, normal murals would have birds instead of bats. Second, in the center was a crystal ball, and in the center of the crystal ball were the powers of a wizard, which constantly shot lighting at the sides of the crystal ball, trying to free itself so that it may return to its master. A chill slipped down TJ's spine. What type of creature would, even if they could, steal a wizard's powers? TJ didn't know of any. He quickly continued onto his first class.

The halls were nearly empty by the time TJ reached the staircase that led to the potions class. He stopped before he went down the staircase and remembered that he forgot his textbook in his dorm. Xander Huston had told him of a shortcut through the atrium to get to the wing of the school where the fourteen-year-old boys were staying. TJ decided to see if that was real or rumor and raced though the classroom hallway being careful not to be seen. He finally reached a hallway with no doors and only picture frames. Suddenly, TJ thought he heard snoring coming from one of the paintings that hung on the wall. "I seriously need to catch up on my sleeping. I'm so tired I think I hear a painting snoring!" TJ laughed to himself and continued on.

Julie, unaware to TJ, was curled up behind one of the paintings in the hallway he'd just passed through, sound asleep and snoring. Julie had used her sweater as a pillow so she wouldn't have to lay her head on the cold, dirt floor of the tunnels. Then, in her dreams, she saw something other than a robbery. She honestly wasn't sure what it was. She saw the tunnels. Every turnoff, every passage; she saw them. Then she saw an exit. It was in the middle of the Headless Woods inside a cabin and hidden behind fishing nets. The cabin was bare. A chimney stood on the end, but that was pretty much it.

Then she saw something else. She saw Joey Munroe, Abby Cooper, Kelsey Dickerson, and two boys Julie didn't know being forced in by two teachers. Julie didn't know which teachers they were because they had their hoods down. The five kids who were being forced in had duct tape over their mouths and chains on their hands. They looked like they hadn't eaten in days, and they were covered in dirt and cuts. The teachers hooked the chains that were already around the kids' wrist to medal loops that stuck out from the walls of the cabin. The duct tape was removed from all of their mouths, and teachers left the cabin after locking the door to the tunnels and the front doors. A green powder began to fall down the chimney, and after it stopped, a mist began to spread though the cabin. The kids began to panic, and Abby sent Kelsey an apologetic glance. They began to scream for help, and that was the end of Julie's dream.

She woke with a start and slowly began to remember where she was. Then she began to put the pieces together. She wrote everything out in the dirt. Kids going missing, teachers saying they never existed, robberies that have to be tied in somehow. And her only guess was that the legendary headless hag's cabin was tied in too, though she couldn't think of how. So the teachers worked for the headless hag? Was that even possible? What was that mist? Nothing made sense. So Julie sat in that freezing, wet tunnel and puzzled over the strange events—that is, until she forgot Abby and Kelsey...again.

TJ had just reached the atrium by that time and was bent over trying to catch his breath. The walls of the atrium were covered in ivy vines, and the floor was just grass and tall weeds. Two stones sat near the right wall. Students had made a habit of sitting on the giant rocks during study period. They also sat on the window ledges of the multiple windows that peered into the atrium. TJ looked in through the closest window and saw Joey Munroe sitting on one of the boulders reading her wizard history book. TJ ducked under a window ledge before she could see him. What if she had? Would she turn him in for not being in class? Even though Joey didn't look up from her book, TJ had a strange feeling she'd seen him, so he left to go the long way to his dorm.

Joey was enjoying her free period studying when she heard voices. She wasn't supposed to be in the atrium during school hour, and she was worried about what would happen if she was caught. She'd heard about what that Lynnel girl did. She'd also heard that she wasn't in class today. Joey quickly took her book and ducked behind a rock. She dared to peek from her hiding place, and she saw Zach and Salfira walk in. They were arguing, and unfortunately for them, Joey heard every word.

"I'm not careful?" Salfira raged. "Oh, like you're even trying to be careful! Do you realize that probably every kid in this god-forsaken place knows that you've walked in the east garden with multiple girls who have just vanished?"

"You know I never came out of the woods except for that one girl that I couldn't take to the hold because of the ogre attack!" Zach spat. "But you came out of the woods with two of your victims!"

"Okay, so we've both been a little reckless," Salfira admitted, lowering her voice. "But listen, I've been getting little suspicious of the Orecs. Do you really think they'll keep their promises?"

During the entire conversation, Joey had been slowly crawling toward the windowsill that was closest to her when she stepped on a twig. The small twig made a huge cracking noise.

"Miss Munroe." Zach smiled an evil smile that the boy Julie thought she knew would never show. "How long have you been in our company?"

Joey tried to run, but Salfira grabbed her in her steel grip. She dragged her over to where Zach stood. Then Zach pulled a crystal ball from his satchel.

TJ had taken so long to get his textbook that he missed his first two classes. When he got back from his dorm, it was in between classes, and all of the kids seemed to be buzzing with news about another disappearance. TJ stopped Adam in his tracks and questioned him without removing his eyes from the other students. "Dude, what's going on?"

"Apparently you weren't the only one who skipped class," Adam explained in a nervous rush. "You know that girl Joey Munroe?"

"Yeah." TJ remembered seeing her studying in the atrium earlier.

"It's like she vanished from the school. The teachers spent all of second period looking for her, and when they couldn't find her, they fanned out into the woods! Can you believe it? Of all places to make an escape! The woods?"

"You think she escaped?" TJ wondered. He had been thinking that she had probably joined the roster of missing people the kids had been keeping.

"Where else—oh, I get it. You think Joey went missing in broad daylight? Someone would have seen what happened to her!" Adam protested.

"I'm not saying that no one did. See if you can find out who else skipped out on class," TJ ordered.

"But what if you were the only one?" Adam blurted out.

"Then we haven't learned anything," TJ answered. "Now we're wasting time. Go get those names!"

Adam rushed off to listen in on gossip, and TJ continued on to his third period class. TJ reached his history class at the end of the hall and entered to find that Ms. Faircloth had started without him.

"Glad you could join us, Mr. Tomas," his teacher spat. "Have you been having fun?"

"No, Ms. Faircloth. It wasn't like that. You see, I forgot my textbook in my dorm—"

"I don't care what excuse you've mustered up. Just sit down and turn your textbook to page six hundred," Ms. Faircloth shot. "Now, as I was saying, who here knows what Umbra is?"

No one raised his or her hand.

"In 1167, magical creatures were exposed. Wizards, living mummies—you name it. They were driven out of the mortal world by a society that had been formed not long after the exposure called the Forever Knights. So the strongest wizards of all time came together and put together all their magic and used it to create their own realm, and they named it Umbra, which still exists to this day. As a matter of fact, I wouldn't be shocked if any of you had ever heard your parents talking about it. Umbra is kind of old fashioned, some of you would say," Ms. Faircloth explained as she rocked back and forth on her heels. "They don't have technology. They still have castles and knights, and the buildings are what you could honestly call ancient."

"So like medieval times?" Tara Spilman wondered.

"Exactly," Ms. Faircloth pointed out.

"If wizards created their own realm for themselves and all the other creatures, why do some of us live here instead of there?" Dylan questioned.

"Because as this world moved on and soon forgot that we were any more than legend, the mortals began to accomplish things that some wizards only dreamed of. So a few wizard families can be found in the mortal world."

Mia Gonzalez raised her hand. "What did the humans accomplish that we couldn't?"

"Good question, Mia. You see, the mortal world moved on while the wizard world stayed frozen in the medieval times by choice," Ms. Faircloth told them. More hands were raised, but Ms. Faircloth waved them down. "We're veering off course. Anyway, the second king to rule Umbra was King Alexander the Aweful. He was given that name because he was proven the worst king who ever ruled. His deeds were comparable to Hitler and Ivan the Terrible. He was assassinated, though, on April 23, 1280, by Orecs," Ms. Faircloth paraphrased from the book.

TJ frowned. "What's an Orec?"

Ms. Faircloth sneered. "Some of your parents did a terrible job of home schooling you. You're supposed to know all of the magical creatures, especially the dangerous ones. No matter. I'll tell you anyway. Orecs make crystal balls and use them to…um, well, they use the crystal balls to steal wizards' powers. Then they absorb the powers to keep them young. Some even use them to make themselves stronger."

"So some wizards can steal others' powers?" Vivian asked, confused.

"No. Wizards and Orecs are completely different creatures," Ms. Faircloth answered.

Conner raised his hand. "So what do Orecs look like?"

"Like wizards," Salfira answered from the doorway. "I'm so sorry. I got lost—"

"I don't want to hear it Miss Matson," Ms. Faircloth spat. "Just take your seat. Even though Miss Matson is late, she is also correct. An Orec could masquerade as a wizard, and no one could ever tell the difference."

"Then how do wizards protect themselves?" Max cried out.

"You will learn that in magic defense," Ms. Faircloth assured. Then she continued her lesson.

After school, Kristine was taking over for Julie in TJ's flying lessons, but they weren't working on flying. Kristine was catching TJ up on what he'd missed in magic defense. "But that makes no sense!" TJ whined.

"It's what Ms. Lindsey said." Kristine sighed. "So we might as well do as the teachers say, right?"

"They say that Orecs are creatures of light, and that the instant dark spell destroys them, but that makes no sense!" TJ repeated. "Orecs are evil, therefore they're creatures of darkness, and the instant sunshine spell destroys them. Did you try to correct Ms. Lindsey?"

"Three kids did, but she wouldn't listen, so let's just do this like she wants us to for now," Kristine shot.

"Fine," TJ agreed. "But while we're out here, in case we're right and she's wrong, I want to practice the instant sunshine spell."

"*Okay*," Kristine gave in. "But you're working on the instant dark first."

"Deal," TJ nodded. He sighed and got into the defensive position they'd been taught in magic defense.

"Wait, TJ!" Kristine interrupted.

"What?"

"You're holding your hand in the wrong direction," she corrected.

"I am not!" he cried.

"Whatever you say. Let's just see you try the spell."

"Even the brightest light cannot recall the darkness that's about to fall. Evil may and might. With instant dark, there is no light!" A shadow shot through TJ's hand right at him and created an explosion. TJ went flying back. When Kristine reached him, he and the area he'd been standing in were covered in ashes.

"TJ?" Kristine whispered in fear. He slowly gained consciousness as he propped himself up on his elbows.

"What happened?"

"You were right," Kristine admitted with a serious face.

"I know. But what went wrong?" TJ questioned.

Kristine smiled a bit. "You weren't holding your hand wrong. You were just standing on the wrong side of it!" She laughed.

TJ smiled. "You think you're so funny. Well, you can stop making jokes now because I admit it. You were right, and I was wrong. Lesson learned. I'll listen to you more often. Now help me to the infirmary," he pleaded.

Kristine helped him up and the two started off.

CHAPTER NINE

Kristine used her hands to try to fan away the smell, but it was no use. She sat behind her bed in her and Julie's room brewing the invisibility potion. She had soon discovered that every part of the poison hemlock Julie had picked smelled like mouse urine. But she stirred the green liquid anyway. She glanced at the sheet of parchment with the recipe on it. She took three leaves of the weeping willow tree and dropped them in the brew. Steam shot up at Kristine and made her even sleepier than before. She glared at the clock on her cell phone and grunted in dismay. It was almost midnight. This was her third attempt at making a correct batch of the potion. She turned back to the bubbling green liquid. She honestly felt sorry for TJ because he would have to drink the chunky slop. *Oh, great,* Kristine thought. Now she was supposed to use part of the deadly nightshade plant. She did as the instructions said and took all the petals from the plant and rolled them into three separate balls and then added them to the disgusting gruel. She stirred the pot some more and sighed. She was done. She put some shrink-wrap over the top of the caldron to contain the stench and then pushed it under her bed.

Kristine stood up, stretched, and then phoned TJ, who had just finished hosting another meeting, "Hey, TJ. It's Kristine."

"Hey, Kristine," TJ replied. "Is it done?"

"Yeah." She sighed as she collapsed on her bed and pulled her gloves off. "So by midnight in two days' time, you'll be invisible. I hope."

"You hope?" TJ nervously questioned.

"You and I both know that there's no guarantee that it's safe or nonpoisonous." Kristine yawned. "I have to go. If I stay awake any longer"—she was interrupted by another yawn—"I'll fall asleep in class tomorrow, and I'm not in the mood to get sent to the dean's office."

"I'm with you there," TJ agreed. They said good night and hung up.

The next day Qwin and Lacy were walking to their first-period class when they ran into Dalton.

"Hey, guys," he greeted. "Sorry about your sis, Qwin."

"What?" she asked, confused.

"Oh, well, you see, the word is that she never made it back to her dorm last night, which means that she's either missing like those eleven other kids or she escaped. Now no offense, but we both know that your sister isn't smart enough to plan an escape."

"I don't know who you heard that from, but my sister isn't missing. Right, Lacy?" Qwin defended.

"Uh, right, but if she isn't missing, then why didn't she return to her dorm yesterday, and where was she during her classes?" Lacy wondered.

"I don't know. Look. After school the three of us will go to the dean's office and ask about her. Okay?"

"Fine," they all agreed. Then they all continued onto class.

Qwin reached Ms. Lindsey's class early and noticed the teacher wasn't there. "Hey, dude, where's the teacher?" Qwin asked Vanessa.

"I don't know. Hey, if your sister's still alive, could she send the dean to a ravine in some unknown part of the world?" Vanessa questioned.

"What?" Qwin cried.

"Oh, well the dean called my uncle an—" Vanessa began.

"No, before the part about the dean," Qwin intersected.

"Oh, you mean the 'hey, if your sister's still alive' part?" Vanessa restated.

"Yeah, that part!" Qwin approved. "But why wouldn't she be alive?"

"Because she's missing?" Vanessa guessed.

"My sister isn't missing!" Qwin yelled. Everyone turned and looked at her, and everything became quiet.

"Look at you kids. You're already settled down before I even arrive." Ms. Lindsey smiled as she neared the class. "Keep that behavior up, and maybe no one will have to go to the office today!" All the kids turned to face her, and class began.

Someone raised his hand. "Is Julie Lynnel missing?"

"Well, that's a strange question. No one from this school is missing, and furthermore, Julian Lynnel has been suspended."

"If no kids are missing, then where's Abby?" Cassidy shot.

"And Chase?" Jordan yelled.

"Let's not forget Alyssa!"

"And Dylan!"

A riot was clearly in the process when someone's deafening voice screamed, "Shut your stupid mouths!" They all turned and found Dr. Culbreth. He stood there looking as angry as ever. "I was just making my rounds, and I decided to stop by and see how PE, flight, and magic defense were going. It's apparently a good thing I did. What is going on?"

"Nothing, sir. I had it all under control," Ms. Lindsey assured him.

"First of all, you can't have nothing under control. Second, whatever was going on, it was obvious you didn't have it under control."

"They were insisting that a bunch of kids who don't exist went to this school," Ms. Lindsey admitted.

The kids started to object again, but Dr. Culbreth only had to yell at them once for them to shut up. "What an absurd and hideous prank! I'd give you all detention, but then we'd need another detention room. I trust that Ms. Lindsey has everything under control from here." He glared at their teacher.

"Yes, sir." She nodded.

Two days later at about midnight, TJ and Kristine sat in Kristine's dorm staring at the bubbling green liquid. "Are you sure you want to do this? Maybe your broom fell asleep. We could go look for it tomorrow," Kristine offered.

"No, I already tried that. It's long past gone. If this gunk doesn't kill me, my dad will."

Suddenly the door to their dorm opened, and the two spun around thinking that they'd been caught. But to their shock, Julie stood in the doorway, unharmed, staring back at them. She noticed them staring at her and slowly walked over to her bed after closing the door to their dorm. She looked back at them again after she sat down. "Did I interrupt something?"

"No, it's just..." Kristine was too stunned to speak.

"We thought you were missing," TJ explained.

"No, I was just locked in the detention room for a while," Julie corrected. The two remained too shocked to talk. Julie tilted her head in confusion and questioned, "You know, if I didn't interrupt anything, why is he here? No offense, TJ."

"We were about to drink the potion and steal the book," TJ assured.

"And by 'we,' he means 'he,'" Kristine added.

"You know, Julie, you could do this for me," TJ almost pleaded.

"No, I don't think I want to get myself in any more trouble this year," Julie answered. "But good luck anyway."

"Wow! Wait, what did they do to you?" TJ cried.

"I told you. They locked me in the detention room for a few days. That's it," Julie repeated.

"Your dad locked you in your room for a week, alone, no results. These people lock you in the detention room for three days, and you never want to do anything again. Something's not right. What aren't you telling us?" TJ persisted.

"Nothing. I'm just tired of getting in trouble," Julie retorted.

"TJ, we're wasting time!" Kristine interrupted. When TJ turned back to her, she whispered, "Don't worry. I'll find out what happened while you're in the library."

TJ stared into the cauldron on the floor. "This is a bad idea," he mumbled to himself. He picked up the cup that he'd conjured up and filled it with the potion. TJ pinched his nose and chugged the cup of slop. A cheetah couldn't have beaten him to the bathroom. The door slammed behind him, and Kristine cast Julie a worried glance. Julie raced to Kristine's side, and the two stood by the bathroom door listing to what sounded like TJ coughing, either that or TJ vomiting.

"TJ?" Julie called nervously.

"Are you okay?" Kristine wondered. The two waited patiently by the door with no response.

"Oh, my God! Kristine, I think you killed him!" Julie cried.

Kristine called for TJ one more time with no response. "Should we open the door?"

"Heck, yeah!" Julie spat. "If you poisoned him, he may not have much time left!"

Kristine rushed forward and through open the bathroom door to find...no one. "Where is he?"

"What do you mean 'where is he'? He's in there, isn't he?" Julie snapped as she stepped into the bathroom to look around. The room was really empty! "Where'd he go?"

"Where'd who go?" TJ's voice floated in from somewhere close.

The girls cried out in shock. Kristine stumbled with a response, "TJ? Where are you?"

"Sitting on the edge of the bathtub. Can't you see me?" TJ responded, confused.

"No!" Julie answered. "TJ, you're invisible!"

"That means the potion worked!" Kristine cried happily. Julie and Kristine high-fived, and TJ cheered.

"Wait!" TJ protested. "How long does the potion last?"

The three fled to the recipe and searched for the answer to TJ's question.

"It says it lasts for two hours, TJ," Kristine explained. "Will that be enough time?"

"Maybe." TJ sighed worriedly.

"Well, good luck," Julie offered. "I'm going to bed."

"You'd better get going," Kristine warned. Kristine couldn't see it, but TJ nodded in agreement. Kristine and Julie watched the door to their dorm open and close by what seemed like itself.

The instant TJ stepped into the hallway, he smelled the burned rubber stench of smoke. He turned and found that smoke was pouring from the eyes of an ominous painting near the end of the hallway. The smoke choked him, and through the grayness that accumulated in front of him, he couldn't see either. He stumbled backward, and suddenly it was as if a giant hand had swept the whole thing away. TJ was so shocked that he raced away from the painting and toward the library. When he reached Window Lane, he slowed to a walk and looked out the windows that looked over the east garden. That's when he saw something he couldn't believe. Smoke floated up into the sky by the lots. It was coming from somewhere deep in the woods. Suddenly it stopped as if it'd been put out. TJ didn't know what to think, but he did know that he needed to get to the library. He closed his eyes and focused, "All this running is making me weary. Take me to the library."

TJ found himself in a dark, dusty, ominous library. He slowly took a step forward, and he heard a loud creak from the floorboard beneath him. He had the overwhelming feeling to look over his shoulder, but when he did, he saw nothing. Across from the doorway, TJ could see one of the five gothic-style windows in the library, and through it he could see a thunderstorm raging outside the school. TJ felt a chill slip down his spine as he continued into the haunting room. He slowly walked down the narrow aisle made by the only two rows of huge bookshelves. Carved into the sides of the shelves were the topics that each shelf held, yet none read spell books.

He reached the back of the room and found there were no other shelves or doorways. TJ left out a long sigh of defeat; there were no spell books. He angrily kicked the wooden wall, causing a cloud of dust to leap at him, but it only took seconds for the wind to blow it away. A thought suddenly came to TJ. *There isn't any wind indoors!* He kicked the wall a second time, and the episode repeated. He moved over and kicked another wall, and dust went airborne, but there was no wind. Just as TJ realized there was a room behind the area he'd kicked, the wall fell off!

TJ jumped behind a bookcase just in time to miss being hit. He watched two of his professors waltz out, each holding a book. They didn't say anything. They just raced out of the library like TJ only wished he could, but he had a job to do. He turned to face the wall, which lay on the floor. Suddenly the wall began to rise up like drawbridges used to. Before the wall got too high off the ground, TJ grabbed the top and swung himself over to the opposite side. Then only a foot or so was left between the wall and the roof. TJ panicked and let go of the top with one hand and reached down and removed his shoe with the other. He quickly stuck it in between the top of the wall and the roof. His hands suddenly slipped, and he fell backward, landing on the hard, wooden floor with a cry of shock. He slowly sat up and looked around to find himself in a room he'd never seen before.

"I keep telling you. They just locked me in the detention room!" Julie sighed. She'd run out of patience with her roommate what felt like a long time ago. Back in the girls' dorm, Kristine kept trying to figure out why Julie was acting weirder than normal.

"I'm not stupid, Julie. I know that you're acting weirder than normal," Kristine repeated for what must have been the billionth time.

"If I tell you, will you quit asking me?" Julie reasoned.

"Yes," Kristine agreed.

"They didn't give me food either," Julie added. "Happy?"

"That's not all," Kristine accused. "I may not know you as well as TJ, but I know that causing trouble is your favorite thing."

Julie had been lying in bed trying to sleep, but she suddenly sat up and turned to Kristine. "They suspended my powers."

"They what?" Kristine whispered in confusion.

"They used some old-fashioned spell to take my powers away, and they just gave them back before they let me go," Julie explained. "I'm not going to let them do it again, and the only way to prevent having them take my powers away is to behave."

"That's impossible," Kristine muttered.

"Good night, crazy," Julie called as rolled over on her side and fell asleep.

TJ slowly stood up and looked around the room. The walls were covered in books from floor to ceiling. A mirror stood in one corner, and there was a large table with multiple chairs surrounding it in the center. The table was covered in book after book, and half, at the most, were thrown open or carelessly left on the floor. He slowly walked over to pick one up and noticed that behind a stack of books stood a small cauldron with steam pouring from the top. "This has to be where they keep the spell books," TJ whispered in excitement. That's when an alarm sounded, and TJ felt his stomach twist into a jungle of knots.

"Intruder! Intruder!" yelled a voice that sounded as if it were coming from inside the room.

TJ spun around and saw a pasty-white face in the mirror yelling that there was an intruder. But the face in the mirror wasn't the only alarming thing he saw. TJ saw his refection. He heard the sound of the wall beginning to lower and dove under the table. TJ listened to the sound of the professors' footsteps as they entered the room in a rush. He watched their feet from his hiding place as they spun around trying to find another person in the library. He slowly scooted forward until he was at the base of the table where he saw a spell book on the floor in front of him. TJ waited for the right moment when they were all still searching the room and then silently dashed out from under the table, grabbed the book he'd seen in front of him and his shoe, which had fallen to the ground as the wall was lowered, and raced along the right wall of the library until he reached the front when he soared beneath the librarian's desk.

"What was that?" TJ heard Mrs. Sawyer cry out from her search post near the back of the library.

"What was what?" Ms. Edwards called from somewhere near the left wall of the library.

TJ was amazed he heard them over the blood pounding in his ears. As the teachers' footsteps neared he quickly cast. "Away from these teachers whose hearts are not warm. Take me to me and Morgan's dorm!"

Dr. Culbreth marched over to the place where Mrs. Sawyer had seen something and looked around. "Under the desk, you say?" She nodded, and he sighed and moved the desk aside to find…no one there.

"I told you so," Ms. Lindsey scolded.

Cassandra was skulking down Window Lane, practically praying that she wouldn't get caught. She was on her way to see what the alarm that had rung earlier was for. There had been an announcement afterward telling them not to leave their dorms, but Cassandra had never been big on rules. She held the kerosene lantern she'd been given at the beginning of the year. It was the only light she had, and she was too lazy to conjure up a flashlight, not to mention the last time she tried to turn her hand into a flashlight, she had to get help changing it back. It was pitch black, and even with the old-fashioned lantern she could barely see where she was going. As if the lane wasn't creepy enough in the day, a cry for help suddenly crept into the long hallway. She could barely hear it, but she could certainly hear it. She turned and hung her lantern out the window and over the east garden. Whoever was yelling was too far away for her to see. "Float high, into the sky!" she cast in a hushed whisper. As if the lantern were on a string, it floated out of her hand and across the east garden, then Cassandra used the hand movement her mom had taught her to stop it over the middle of the east garden.

That's when she saw it. The people the lantern revealed probably didn't notice the lantern because of how little light shone. They most likely thought the moon had just come out from behind the storm clouds. Cassandra saw a boy and a girl, both probably students. They were walking backward, slightly bent over, as they dragged another girl to what appeared to be the woods. The girl being kidnapped looked no older than ten, maybe eleven years old. Their faces were not clearly visible because of how little light there was, but the girl's hair color was. Both one of the kidnapper's hair and the victim's were blonde. Both the boy and the girl were holding one of the victim's hands as they pulled against her.

Cassandra was sick at the sight, and the thought of the fact she was witnessing a kidnapping. She knew she didn't have time to get a teacher. If she was going to help the girl, she had to do it herself. She knew what she had to do, but she also knew the risk. She stuck her fingers in her mouth and let out a loud whistle. Everything in the east garden suddenly stood still, as if someone had hit the pause button on the remote. In seconds, Cassandra's broom had flown to her side in answer to its master's whistle. Then as if someone had hit the fast-forward button on the remote, everything in the garden was moving again. The kidnappers must have been pulling a lot harder because they were now dragging the girl through the dirt and flowers as she bucked and kicked like a fish that had been taken out of water, and she was screaming a lot louder.

Cassandra mounted her broom and raced down into the garden and was going straight at the criminals who were only a few feet from the woods. She missed them, and when she was a few inches away from the tree trunks, she pulled a one-eighty and spun to face the kidnappers and victim. Before she could see their faces, the boy used a spell to shoot down her lantern, and within seconds, the garden was covered in darkness. Something heavy came down and knocked Cassandra off her broom and into the mud. Before she could get up, it came at her again and hit her hard in the head, causing a loud crack. Whenever she tried to sit up, she felt like she was going to throw up. If the lights came back on, Cassandra couldn't see them.

The morning sunrise awoke Cassandra with a start. She slowly sat up, trying to remember where she was. That's when she remembered the incident from the previous night. She looked at her surroundings and saw a few yards behind her was her broom, which was broken in half and unmoving. She looked at her reflection in a puddle and saw she was caked with mud. She walked a few more yards forward and found something unfamiliar in the grass.

It was a silver, flower-shaped locket. Across the front, the sentence "To yourself be true" was engraved. Cassandra carefully opened it and saw the faded picture inside. There was a man and a woman sitting on picnic blanket in what looked like a desert. There was a little boy sitting inside the picnic basket with a stupid grin on his face. There were also two little girls, one a baby, and one was four or five years old. The woman was holding the baby, and the man had the little girl in his lap. The little girl was trying to get up and tackle the boy. It was one goofy family portrait.

There was a piece of notebook paper wedged into the opposite side of the locket. Cassandra took it out and unfolded the note and read the sloppy writing that had apparently been written in a hurry. It read:

> To whom it may concern:
>
> I've learned a key clue in the mystery to where the kids are going. Despite the fact that I've told no one that I know, I think they know that I know. I think I may be the next to go missing because, after all, a secret's not a secret if someone

knows. If I do go missing, tell my sister, Julie. Or better yet, give her this note. She has to know that the people behind this are—

It looked as if she had run out of time or something and had to hide the letter quickly. But whatever happened, the note was never finished. So this girl solved the mystery and left a note that didn't tell anyone what it is in a locket that holds a key clue to who she was? That was pretty smart. Well, sort of. All Cassandra knew for sure was that she had to find this Julie, whoever she was. It would have been helpful for that girl to give her sister a last name.

CHAPTER TEN

"I'm telling you I know what I saw!" Cassandra defended herself. The teachers had retrieved her from the east garden about an hour after she'd woken up. But after she'd told them what she'd seen, she'd been ridiculed by the teachers, yelled at, and called a liar. Then when she produced the locket, she'd been called a thief and a forger. But since no one was missing any jewelry, they couldn't punish her for that. They had given her three months of detention for so many things that Cassandra couldn't remember half of them. But what she did know was that she didn't deserve anything that happened to her. Though every argument she'd had with the teachers had brought them back to where they were now, discussing what had happened the night before. Cassandra could punch her professors right in their kissers for everything they'd been putting her through. But she knew that they wouldn't give her a shred of their time anymore if she did, and anyone could tell that even now they hated her.

"How do you know that you weren't dreaming?" Dr. Culbreth ventured.

"Because even if I was, why do I have a bump on the back of my head where they hit me? Or maybe you have thought of a tie to me dreaming and my broom being broken?" Cassandra spat. She really, really hated these people.

"That is it, young lady! I will not have you in my office any second longer! We have already given you your punishment, so get out!"

Cassandra had never been so happy to leave any place in her entire life! It was then she decided that she was definitely going to prove those teachers wrong. She was going to find Julie and tell her what just happened, and then she was going to help her pick up where her sister left off—solving the mystery of the missing kids. But she still couldn't believe the dean. It was like he didn't even care! She took out the locket again and looked at the portrait. Which was Julie? Cassandra guessed that is was impossible to tell and went to her dorm. She found McKenzie sitting on her bed e-mailing her mom back home.

She turned toward her roommate, and a look of relief covered her face. "Thank God. Do realize how shocked I was when I woke up at three this morning and you weren't here? Do you think that I wanted to spend my entire morning knocking on everyone's door asking if they'd seen you? What happened to you?"

"I went out to see what the alarm was," Cassandra began.

"What alarm?" McKenzie wondered.

"You slept through it," Cassandra answered. "And I saw this girl being kidnapped, so I flew down on my broom to help her, but one of the two kidnappers knocked me out. I woke up, and the dean ordered me to the office, which is where I'm coming from now."

McKenzie whistled. "Wow. Who was the girl being kidnapped?"

"I don't know. Look at this!" Cassandra produced the silver locket, and McKenzie took it from her hand and opened it. Cassandra waited patiently as her roommate read the note and looked at the portrait. She was silent a long time, then she looked at Cassandra and down again.

"This girl could have saved us all, and she slipped through our fingers. Not only that, but Julie, this girl's sister, could save us all, and we don't even know where to start," McKenzie sighed, disappointed.

A look of realization crossed Cassandra's face. "The enrollment records! This girl was as young as it gets when it comes to students who attend this school, and if she told us to find Julie, that must mean Julie's a student here. So if Julie's a student, she's in the enrollment records! We can find her that way!" The girls rejoiced.

"Not only that, but we have a picture of her!" McKenzie cried out happily.

"We do?" Cassandra questioned, confused.

"If the baby in this portrait is the one who solved the mystery, then the little girl is Julie!" McKenzie explained. "All we have to do is find all the Julies in the school and decide which one this little girl grew up to be!" McKenzie and Cassandra smiled. McKenzie turned to Cassandra, her eyes asking if she was ready to do the spell.

"I have to do it?" Cassandra asked unsure.

"We both have to. It takes a lot of power to do the spell, but our combined efforts should do the trick," McKenzie assured her. The girls stood side by side and hand in hand.

The girls took a deep breath and then recited, "Let the names of every child who's learned here be known. Let the names of every child who's been here be shown. Bring forth the names of those who've passed and those who are still here. Let the names of every child who's learned here be known!" A blinding flash of light filled the room for at least three seconds. When the girls opened their eyes, they saw floating blue letters. The names were floating all around the room! *There are so many*, McKenzie observed. And she was right. The girls couldn't move without bumping into one.

"There aren't this many people in the school!" Cassandra cried.

"That's because the spell calls for the names of every kid who's ever learned here. Past and present," McKenzie clarified. The two groaned. There were so many names! It was going to take all week to find all the Julies! And they couldn't even make it to the door! "Nice," McKenzie mumbled. "If anyone asks after we save all the kids, you can take credit for the enrollment records."

"Are you sure? You can take some credit too."

"Let me just say what we're both thinking: this was a dumb idea," McKenzie realized. "We should have just stuck with the picture."

"What about this one?" TJ wondered. TJ, Julie, Kristine, and Morgan were sitting on the floor in the guys' dorm in between the beds looking at the spell book that TJ had swiped. They had been doing so all day because, for some reason, there was no school that day. They had heard that a girl had been found in the east garden—again. Although, luckily, this time it didn't seem to be Julie. TJ had pointed out a lot of spells, but Kristine had pointed out they were all for finding lost pets, not lost brooms.

"I don't know about that one. My dad tried that one once, and it turned him blue for a month," Kristine told. One thing every wizard knew about casting spells was it won't always turn out just right if not pronounced right or used for the precise situation. In that case it can cause injury, do things wrong, or worse. And every wizard knew that one thing from experience.

"No, thank you. I don't care if your old man is gonna chop you up and hide you in a bucket. I don't think I want to change color, even for a month," Morgan objected. No one disagreed, and they kept looking. They turned five more pages before Morgan pointed out another spell. "Would that one get his broom back without causing any side effects?"

"Do you want it straight? Or would you prefer a pretty little lie?" Julie returned.

"What do you know?" Morgan snapped. "Didn't the letters on your last report card read D-, D-, D-, D-, F?"

"Hey, one of those was a D- plus!" Julie shot back.

"She's got a point," Kristine intervened. "That spell turned my cat inside out."

"Way to go, Julie. That D's the best grade you've ever gotten," TJ joked. "How about this one?" he asked as they turned another page.

"Hey, that might work!" Kristine cried.

"Seriously?" TJ shouted with glee.

"Maybe," Kristine admitted. "It's the only one so far that's been worth a shot."

"So are you going to try it?" Julie and Morgan questioned at the same time.

"Do you want to do it?" Kristine asked TJ uneasily. He was quiet for a long time.

"Maybe you should try it. You're better at spells than I am," TJ nervously replied.

"Okay." Kristine sighed uncomfortably. She didn't want to cast the spell. What if she did it wrong? What would be the consequences? What if she turned inside out?

"I'm just gonna take myself out of the line of fire for this one," Morgan announced as he quickly climbed to his feet and started to slowly back out of the room. Then he suddenly turned around and ran into the hallway, closing the door behind him. He obviously didn't think she could do it right. She looked up at TJ and Julie, and that's when Julie suddenly got up, and as quickly as Morgan had been gone, so was she.

Kristine's eyes fell on TJ. "Do you think I can do it? Or do you want to head out to?"

"Do you want me to go?" TJ wondered.

"Do you want to go?" Kristine asked.

"I guess not." TJ sighed. "Let's get this over with."

Kristine watched as TJ squeezed his eyes shut, and she took a deep breath. Not even TJ thought she could do it. It's not that she wasn't good at casting spells, but she had never done any that were in a spell book. Spell books were reserved for advanced wizards. "At midnight, a broom roams. At midnight, a broom comes home. If it's not found, someone will be in pain. Return this broom to Window Lane!" There was a huge gust of wind that sent TJ flying into the door. Then nothing.

"Well." TJ sighed as he opened his eyes and rubbed the back of his head where it'd cracked against the door. "That could have been worse. Too bad it didn't work, though."

"Not necessarily," Kristine corrected. "We won't know until midnight. That's when the book says that the spell's supposed to take effect."

"So that wasn't it?" TJ wondered.

"I hope not," Kristine answered.

"We should tell Morgan and Julie that they can come in now," Kristine suggested.

"Yeah," TJ agreed as he shakily stood up.

"Are you okay?" Kristine wondered.

"I think so." TJ sighed. "Thanks for asking."

They opened the door and found the two sitting in the hallway impatiently. When they came into the hallway, Julie and Morgan leaped to their feet and questioned in unison, "Well? Did you cast the spell right? Does TJ have his broom? Were there any side effects?"

"Whoa, one question at a time. And in answer to all those questions, we'll find out at midnight."

Meanwhile, Cassandra and McKenzie were busy eliminating names from the floating mess of letters that zoomed around their dorm. "Do you know how to speed read?" McKenzie wondered. "If so, this could be going a lot faster."

"No, my older brother does, but I don't. In my opinion, you have to be a nerd to want to learn to speed read," Cassandra explained.

"Well, I don't think your opinion applies to this situation, now does it?" she snapped.

"Sorry," Cassandra muttered.

"Does your older brother attend here? If so, we could just call him on the phone and ask him to come down here and help us," McKenzie suggested.

"He doesn't go here," Cassandra revealed. "He's twenty-five."

"Oh. Do you see him often?"

"No." She sighed simply.

"Why not?" McKenzie questioned.

"He's a Marine Corp sniper. Spends most his time overseas," Cassandra answered. "I've always hated him. Never thought I'd miss him when he left."

"Do you?" McKenzie asked.

Cassandra hesitated. "I'm not sure."

McKenzie frowned. "Do you even like him?"

"I guess he has his moments." Cassandra sighed. "Whenever I realized there was a chance I might die here, the weirdest thing happened. I started to feel worried, but not for myself. It was almost like I was worried I'd never see him again."

"You were," McKenzie assumed. "You said his name in your sleep a few days ago."

"You're lying," Cassandra accused without looking away from the names that she was erasing after making sure they weren't important.

"Is his name Daniel?"

"Yeah," she muttered.

"You said his name."

"Can we get back to the enrollment records?" Cassandra insisted.

"You think your brother's a nerd?"

"And?"

"It would take a nerd to finish all this before classes tomorrow, so think like Daniel. What would he do?" McKenzie wondered.

"Eliminate every name that doesn't have a first or middle name pertaining to Juliann, Julian, Juliette, Junelle, or Juliana," Cassandra said.

"That's what we're doing now!"

"He'd think of a way to do it faster," Cassandra grumbled.

"Like how?" McKenzie cried.

Cassandra's eyes lit up. "I know what we can do! Spell improvisation!"

"That's why God invented nerds." McKenzie smiled after finally finding a quicker way to find this girl's name. McKenzie took a deep breath and tried. "A Julie is who we need to find, but we're running a bit behind. Shed some light on which we're looking for, and open for us every possible door!" Suddenly the number of names decreased until there was only a thirtieth of what used to be.

"Thank goodness for spell improvisation!" Cassandra cried.

"No, thank goodness for your ability to think like a nerd!" McKenzie corrected as she grabbed a pen and a piece of paper from her bed. "Now stop staring at me like you'd like to slit my throat, and start writing down names and dorm numbers!"

Cassandra did as she was told, but she also didn't speak again for the rest of the evening.

Later that night, TJ, Kristine, and Julie were standing in Window Lane, each monitoring a section of windows. TJ glanced at his watch. "Thirty seconds until midnight."

"Okay, guys. Keep your eyes wide open," Kristine demanded. She was monitoring the window in the middle. TJ watched the ones to the left and Julie to the right.

"Three, two, one," TJ counted down.

That's when, before any of them were even sure what was going on, TJ's broom soared in through the window in the very center of all the windows in the entire hall and smashed Kristine smack in the face. TJ lunged at the broom, and Julie rushed to help her roommate.

After what felt worse to TJ than a professional wrestling match, he had his broom pinned to the dirt-covered floor, and with a wrinkle of his nose, the broom was in the shed with all the others. "How is she?" he asked as he rushed to Kristine's side. She was slowly sitting up. Julie's hand was behind her supporting her back. A river of blood poured from her nose.

"How many fingers am I holding up?" Julie held her other hand out in front of Kristine and held up two fingers.

"Two," she managed.

"What's your name?" TJ questioned.

"Kristine."

"What's the date?" Julie asked.

"October the eleventh, two thousand nine," Kristine answered. "My head hurts so badly. What happened?"

"We'll tell you on the way back to your dorm," TJ assured. "But we have to head back now. Someone could have heard the noise and could be on their way now."

Kristine used Julie and TJ for support as they helped her back to her dorm.

CHAPTER ELEVEN

Julie, Kristine, and TJ were in the west garden. TJ was practicing broom flying, and once again, things weren't going so great. *At least this time*, Julie thought, *no one is getting hit in the face by his broom.* She cast a quick glance to Kristine. Her entire forehead was bruised. Kids had asked what happened, but they thought it a miracle the teachers hadn't said a word. She started watching TJ again, who was going little higher than he had before. To be honest, though, Julie had seen fish fly higher. She never meant to be mean about his flying skills, but he was only a few inches off the ground. *But hey*, she thought, *a few is better than one and a half.*

Julie started daydreaming when suddenly Kristine cried out. Julie turned her attention to her and then to TJ. And when she looked at TJ, she saw what the problem was. He wasn't there! She looked up, and to her shock, she saw him! His broom kept going higher and higher until suddenly he was equal with a window on the second story! That's when, in Julie's opinion, the nightmare began. The broom raced through the window!

She heard cries of shock from inside the school, and she could only imagine the chaos unfolding in that school. She and Kristine popped to their feet and raced inside. Once they reached Window Lane, Julie and Kristine decided to split up. Kristine would search for TJ and his broom in the tower, and Julie would guard the entrance to the rest of the school.

Kristine started going up the next flight of stairs when suddenly TJ, still clinging to the broom for dear life, came shooting right at her. She ducked at just the right second, and the broom flew over her. "Julie!" Kristine shrieked in panic.

Julie spun around and ducked just in time. TJ was still on his broom, so they couldn't use spells to shoot him down; neither of them had good enough aim. Kristine was by Julie's side in a matter of two seconds. They watched together in horror as TJ's broom just kept going through the hall. That's when suddenly two girls appeared at the end of the hallway and didn't see TJ coming right at them. Julie and Kristine looked at each other in terror, and together they cried, "Look out!"

The other two girls looked up in shock. The one on the right managed to hit the ground in time, but the other girl was frozen in fear. She managed to raise her hands to protect her face in time, but that only made it worse. The broom flew right at her, and a charm bracelet she'd been wearing got caught on the head of the broom. Next thing she knew she was being dragged along for the ride. The broom suddenly made a u-turn and flew right back at Julie and Kristine! They cried out in shock and ducked. The broom sailed right over them, but the girl's shoes managed to kick them in the face. The broom flew down the staircase. The girl who been walking with TJ's passenger ran over to them.

"What just happened?" she screamed at them. "Where's he taking Cassandra?"

"Flight lesson gone out of control," Julie explained. "They headed in the direction of the west garden. We'll just follow them there. Don't worry. I'm sure Cassandra is fine—" Julie didn't get to finish. The girl shoved Kristine and Julie on to the ground and raced down the stairs. The girls propped themselves up on their elbows. Julie turned to Kristine. The girls' hair was a mess, all over their faces and eyes. "Do you know what I like the most about this place?"

"No," Kristine mumbled as they pulled themselves to their feet and brushed their hair out of their faces.

"Nothing. I absolutely hate this place," Julie grumbled as they raced down the steps after the runaway broom.

When they reached the west garden, they saw the girl who'd shoved them down helping her friend out of the mud and TJ apologizing profusely from where he was standing up. He held his broom tightly so that it wouldn't get away.

Julie and Kristine raced up to him. "Are you okay?"

"Is *he* okay?" the girl who'd shoved them down snapped. "Cassandra could have been killed!"

"Look, you little—" Kristine covered her roommate's mouth just in time.

"What she means to say is we're sorry. TJ didn't mean for his broom to get caught on your bracelet," Kristine corrected.

"No way! If I had meant to say that—" Kristine quickly covered her roommate's mouth again.

"It's okay," Cassandra said. "I'm sorry for my roommate's behavior. She has anger management problems."

"So does she." Julie gestured to Kristine, who elbowed her in the gut. "She's Kristine."

"That's McKenzie." Cassandra smiled.

"I still exist," TJ shot.

"Sorry," Julie called. "I was just making nice with McKenzie and her friend, who you nearly killed!"

TJ just shook his head and went to go put his broom away.

"So that must be TJ." Cassandra sighed.

"And you must be Cassandra." Julie nodded. "And I'm Julie."

"*You're* Julie?" Cassandra and McKenzie cried in shock.

"Wow. I guess I didn't know how many people knew I sent Mrs. Sawyer to that ravine." Julie blushed.

"That was you?" McKenzie gasped.

"If you don't know me from that, how do you know me?"

"Listen, Julie." McKenzie led her over to the stairs that went into the west tower. The four girls sat down. "I've been looking for you."

"I didn't do it," Julie said on reflex. "What didn't I do?"

"We're not accusing you of something," Cassandra explained. She wondered if she knew her little sister was missing. She hoped she did, and then she wouldn't have to tell her the bad news. Giving people bad news was what she was worst at. She brushed a strand of her long brown hair that went to her back out of her face. Her dark brown eyes filled with sadness as she remembered watching Julie's sister struggling. "Do you have a sister?"

"Yeah, my little sister, Qwin," Julie answered. "She didn't show up to school today. People were saying the worst things. Do you know what happened to her?"

"The other night I snuck out of my dorm to see what the alarm was about—"

"That was TJ's bad," Kristine revealed.

"Anyway, when I was crossing Window Lane, I saw your sister in the east garden," Cassandra began.

Julie and Kristine stood up. Julie shouted, "No, you're wrong! She would never go in there, not in a million years, not in a billion years!"

"She wasn't there willingly. She was being kidnapped. I'm sorry." Cassandra watched the two girls sit down.

Julie wiped a tear from her eye and glared at Cassandra for a long time. "Who?"

"I don't know. I'm sorry," Cassandra explained and apologized again.

"Are you telling me you can recognize my sister who you've never even met in the dark, but you can't recognize her kidnappers, who you might actually know?" Julie shouted through her tears.

"I didn't know who your sister was until…Let me just tell you what happened," Cassandra pleaded.

"I don't want to know what happened. I want to know where my sister is!" Julie screamed.

Cassandra told the story anyway. "I saw three people in the east garden. I couldn't make out any faces, but I could make out a boy and a girl about our age forcing her through the garden toward the trees." Cassandra told the whole story. She even told them about how she found out her name was Julie.

"So my sister's in the woods?" Julie persisted.

"Well, maybe. But do you have any idea why all these kids are going missing? I mean, we thought maybe your sister had said something to you. Anything like that?" McKenzie wondered.

"She didn't say anything to me." Julie sighed as they all stood up. By then, TJ had joined them, and he stood up with Julie and Kristine. "I'm sorry." Julie sighed. "I wish I could tell you what you want to know, but I've got to find my sister." Suddenly Julie broke out in a cold-sweat run for the tree line.

"Julie!" Kristine, TJ, McKenzie, and Cassandra raced after her. They kept calling her name. They knew she could hear them, but she kept on running. The only thing on Julie's mind was her sister and how she had to help her before it was too late.

TJ managed to tackle her right at the tree line—so close in fact, that Julie's head smashed into a pine tree.

"Julie! Are you all right?" TJ rolled her over and saw the tiny drops of blood running from a cut on her head that the collision with the pine tree had caused. "Oh, wow. Julie, I'm sorry! I didn't mean to hurt you. I was just trying to stop you." Now TJ was on his feet, and he was offering her a hand up.

Kristine, McKenzie, and Cassandra had reached them then. And all four of them—TJ, Kristine, Cassandra, and McKenzie—watched Julie roll around in the leaves and pine straw that painted the grass golden at the tree line, sobbing. She was holding her head in her hands, and to her friends' shock, she was screaming, "Go away! Get out of my head!"

"Oh, my God," Kristine breathed.

"I'll get the nurse," Cassandra assured.

She rushed off, and McKenzie got down her knees beside Julie on the ground. Julie was still screaming the same thing over and over again. McKenzie sighed and started to reach out for her.

"What are you going to do?" Kristine questioned.

"She needs to stop rolling around so we can see how badly she's hurt or at the very least stop the bleeding," Kristine explained as she suddenly grabbed both Julie's wrists in her hands and pinned them to the ground. Julie fought back, and she looked to TJ and Kristine for help.

"I can't believe I'm doing this," Kristine whispered as she and TJ slowly squatted down to the pine needles, and TJ pinned his best friend's legs while Kristine gently reached out and pinned her shoulders to the ground.

Julie kept screaming, "Go away!" Soon her tears formed rivers that flooded down her face causing her makeup to run. It seemed she never tired. She just kept fighting.

"Where's Cassandra with the nurse?" McKenzie shouted. She had to shout to be heard over Julie's screams. McKenzie wanted so badly to reach out and stop the blood from pouring down Julie's face, but she was too busy keeping Julie's hands pinned to the ground. Soon McKenzie could see tears coming from TJ and Kristine as well. *They can't stand seeing their friend like this*, McKenzie realized. That's when she realized something was wrong. Julie wasn't fighting anymore. She wasn't even screaming. McKenzie looked to TJ and Kristine. They'd noticed it too.

Slowly they let go of Julie and stared at her, quickly beginning to worry that Julie was dead. She lay there in the leaves and pine straw unmoving. Her head was turned to the left, and her eyes were closed. Her knees were bent to the side, and her mouth was both closed and frowning. There were bruises on her wrists where McKenzie was forced to restrain her. TJ bent down and wiped the blood from her face. She wasn't bleeding anymore. One of them would have taken her pulse if they weren't so scared that she wouldn't have one.

"Oh, my!" a voice called from behind them. They spun around and saw Cassandra had arrived with the nurse. The nurse rushed forward and kneeled down beside Julie. Cassandra stood a few feet behind them mouth open wide.

"Did you kill her?" Cassandra managed in a terrified whisper.

"No, she's got a pulse," the nurse announced. They all sighed, relieved. The nurse was young the kids noticed. Well, young compared to the teachers anyway. Her brown and white hair was pulled back into a bun, and she was very thin. Her eyes were the brightest blue any of them had ever seen, and she wore a plain white nurse's uniform. "What did you do to this girl?" she cried as she put a butterfly bandage on the cut on Julie's head that had been bleeding so profusely only moments ago.

"Um…" TJ was trying to find the words to explain when he thought he heard voices. He turned to the three girls that stood beside him and saw they were looking behind them toward Window Lane. TJ turned and saw that Window Lane was filled with kids. All had turned away from the east garden and were now looking at the ruckus taking place in the west garden.

Some kids had conjured up binoculars, and some were simply shielding their eyes; others were sitting on the windowpanes, but most were just leaning out the windows trying to see who was lying in the pine straw and grass.

"What did you do to this girl?" the nurse repeated as she gently lifted Julie out of the grass.

"I tackled her, and when she fell, her head hit a tree," TJ admitted after turning away from the school.

"Were you trying to kill her?" the nurse spat.

"No, I was trying to stop her from going in the woods," he explained.

Suddenly the nurse poofed them into a huge infirmary. It wasn't as big as a football field, but it came close. There were multiple beds lining each wall. The bricks that made the walls were uneven and plain and gray. The beds were plain and white with an optional white curtain that could be drawn around each bed. There were tables beside each bed. Some had medicine, and some didn't.

"Where are we?" McKenzie wondered.

"The infirmary," the nurse answered as if it'd been obvious. "On the second floor of the school. The library is just down the hall."

"Oh." Cassandra sighed.

The nurse set Julie own on a bed in the middle of the long line of beds. "So tell me what happened to her again from the beginning."

The kids automatically felt respect for the nurse. She was the first adult in this school who had ever wanted to hear what the kids had to say. Cassandra and McKenzie glared at Kristine. "You should tell her. We weren't there in the beginning."

So Kristine told the nurse the whole story, starting when Julie, TJ, and she first showed up in the west garden that afternoon for TJ's flying lessons.

When she finished, the nurse used Velcro straps on the side of the bed to restrain Julie's hands.

"Do you really think that's necessary?" Kristine asked.

"I don't know," the nurse admitted. "But I'll tell you what I think. I think that someone gave her a potion that allowed him or her to get inside her head and make her think what they wanted her to think. What happened in the west garden was when you told Julie her sister was kidnapped. Whoever slipped her the potion wanted her to forget that she knew her sister was gone. Are you following?"

"Sort of," McKenzie replied. "Keep going."

"The reason such a bizarre episode took place in the west garden is because Julie fought back. She didn't want to forget her sister to a point that she was able to break the hold whoever slipped her the potion had on her, even though it nearly scrambled her brain in doing so. When she was screaming 'go away' in the west garden, it wasn't at *you*. It was at whoever was in her head," the nurse finished.

"So she's not crazy, and it's not my fault?" TJ clarified.

"Correct." The nurse nodded.

"Then why did you restrain her hands?" Kristine asked.

"Because," the nurse explained, "whoever did this to her may not be gone yet."

"Is there any way to trace the potion?" McKenzie wondered.

"No." The nurse sighed. "No, I'm sorry. Now you need to go and let the poor girl rest."

The children nodded and slowly vanished to the sanctity of their dorms.

CHAPTER TWELVE

Julie tried to roll over but felt something restraining her hands and keeping her in place. She tried to open her eyes to see where she was, but she felt too weak and instead slowly drifted back to sleep. That's when she had another dream.

She saw the four of them, TJ, Kristine, Cassandra, and McKenzie, all sitting in the waiting room to the dean's office. "You can come in now," he called. The four of them rose and silently proceeded into his office as if they were walking in a funeral procession.

"Where is she?" Kristine asked before the dean could inquire what was wrong.

"Where's who?" the dean asked, for a moment looking truly confused, but that moment didn't last too long.

"Qwin Lynnel," Cassandra hissed. The dean gave her the evil eye, no doubt remembering how she claimed to have witnessed a student's kidnapping.

"At her home in Amarillo, Texas. Her father called and said that it was a mistake to send her away and that he'd like to give her another chance," he lied. "Any other questions?" The dean scowled.

"No, sir," McKenzie answered through her teeth. Then the four, who looked rather angry, turned and left the office.

"They've got Qwin." TJ sighed miserably after they closed the door behind themselves.

"What are we going to do?" McKenzie wondered.

"Keep trying to put the pieces together," TJ decided. "And watch our sixes, because that's all we can do."

"Our what?" McKenzie wondered.

"That's the military term for 'watch your back,'" Cassandra clarified.

Then the dream ended, and Julie woke up again. This time she managed to open her eyes. She stared up at the ceiling of the infirmary.

"Where..." she mumbled.

"The school infirmary," the nurse informed her.

"Why?" she muttered.

"You were slipped a belief potion," the nurse explained. "But we flushed it out of your system. You should be fine now."

"What?" Julie wondered as she sat up on her elbows. Then she felt the curious feeling that something was holding her wrist back. She looked down and saw the restraints. "What the—"

"Those were precautionary. I wasn't sure what state of mind you'd be in when you woke up," the nurse explained.

"Well, obviously my state of mind is fine now." Julie glared. "You can take these things off my wrist now."

The nurse stood up from her seat on a stool next to Julie's bed and unsnapped the restraints.

"Thanks." Julie sighed as she lay back down. "I feel like crap."

"To be expected." The nurse sighed.

"I have a headache too."

"I'd be shocked if you didn't."

"Do you keep up with the gossip around the school?"

"I try."

"What's the word on Qwin Lynnel?" Julie wondered.

"That she went home," the nurse revealed.

"Okay. Thanks," Julie replied. She snapped her fingers, and her laptop appeared on her lap. She was still feeling week from when she hit her head on the tree, so she decided not to over work herself by using a spell to send this message. *I guess these things* are *good for something,* she thought as she opened up the laptop. The nurse got up and walked to her desk in the back of the room as Julie logged into her e-mail account that she'd finally broke down and set up when her mortal friends from school kept asking for her e-mail; Julie had been worried she'd look too strange if she had said she didn't have one. Twelve e-mails from her friends back in Amarillo. Twelve e-mails she would *eventually* read. There were no e-mails from Nathan, her older brother who also had an email account for the same reason, but she wasn't surprised. She knew before she set foot on the train for this stupid boarding school that she would never get any attempts at communication from him. But he was about to get one from her.

> Hey idiot,
>
> Yeah, I know I'm the last person you want to hear from right now. But seriously, it's an emergency. You don't believe me? Well, then you can call the school and verify that I'm writing you from the school infirmary. And the person who put me here kidnapped Qwin. You don't believe me about that either? Call the school and pretend to be a concerned parent from South Dakota or something and ask for Qwin Lynnel. They'll tell you her dad called her home. I know writing you won't bring her back, but since the only phones here are tapped, I think Qwin would want me to ask you to call the wizard police. Will you at least think about it?
>
> Julie

She sighed. She didn't know if Nathan would actually do anything, but writing him to call the police was better than sitting around doing nothing. She just hoped it would be enough, although she had a feeling it wouldn't be.

Nathan had just gotten home from school; his dad wouldn't be home for three more hours, so he tossed his book bag on the ground next to the couch. He violently yanked out his laptop and plopped down on the couch, then snatched up the TV remote and turned on a football game. He almost missed the noise of his sisters blaring their iPods next to him. He definitely didn't miss them hogging the couch; he greedily kicked his feet up and stretched out. He opened his laptop and turned it on, and then he checked his e-mails. That's when he couldn't believe his eyes. He had an e-mail from his *sister!* Now that would vaguely make sense if it were Qwin, but not Julie. No, this made no sense. He decided he'd humor her and read it. He scowled and nearly deleted the e-mail without reading it after seeing the greeting. "Hey idiot" it read. But then he read the rest, and he forgot about the greeting. He took his feet down and turned off the TV. He took his laptop off his lap, and he put his elbows on his knees and his face in his hands. *What am I going to do?* he wondered. And it was a good question. He glanced at the laptop one last time and thought, *Well, it couldn't hurt to try.* So then he picked up the phone.

Dr. Culbreth was sitting in his chair behind his desk when his phone rang. "Hello, this is the—"

"Yeah, I know who I'm talking to. This is James Thornton. I'm calling because I need to talk to Qwin Lynnel."

"She's been called home by her parents," Dr. Culbreth lied.

"Then can I talk to Julie Lynnel?"

"She's in the school's infirmary," Dr. Culbreth disclosed. "May I take a message?" The dean took the phone away from his ear when he realized Mr. Thornton had hung up. He wondered why he'd asked for the Lynnel girls. *Oh, well,* he thought. *Does it matter?*

Nathan quickly dialed his father's cell phone number. He didn't care that his sisters were jerks or liars or that whatever was going on they were getting what they deserved. He forgot that all because his sisters were in trouble. He put the phone to his ear and listened to its ring. "Dad?"

"Nathan?" his father answered. "What's wrong?"

"Something's wrong at the school," he gushed in a single breath.

"What school?"

"The ones my sisters are at!"

"How could you possibly know that?" he asked.

"I called," Nathan explained.

"*You?*" His father laughed. "Called *Julie* and *Qwin?*"

"I called and asked to speak to them, and they said Julie was in the infirmary and—"

"What? Why is Julie—"

"Doesn't matter! Well, it matters, but oh, you know what I mean! Just listen! They said Qwin was with us!"

"What?"

"That's my point!"

"Why'd you call the school in the first place?" his father questioned. "I mean, I'm glad you did, but you barely talk to your sisters when they're at home."

"I got an e-mail from Julie. She said that she was in the infirmary and that Qwin had been kidnapped, and that if I didn't believe her, I could call the school pretending to be someone else and they'd tell me Julie was in the infirmary and Qwin was with us, which they did."

"Call the Wizard Police. I'm on my way home."

Kristine, TJ, Cassandra, and McKenzie were leaving the dean's office. Suddenly, Lacy raced around the corner so fast she bumped into Kristine and knocked her onto her back. Kristine cried out in shock at the same moment that Lacy cried out in pain as she slammed into the marble tile floor. "What the heck?" Kristine yelled.

TJ helped them both up, and they all turned their attention to Lacy. She seemed flustered. She was shaking slightly and had blood dripping from the corner of her mouth. "Oh my God. Lacy, are you okay?"

"I was in the grand hall a few minutes ago, and I saw Zach slip something into Tina's drink! I tried to warn her, but she wouldn't believe me! So I tried to confront Zach—"

TJ interrupted Lacy. "Alone? Lacy, do you know how stupid that is?" he practically yelled as he reached out and grabbed her by the shoulders.

"Yeah, I know," she replied as she shook his hands off her shoulders. "But I wasn't thinking."

"Did he do this to you?" Kristine asked as she whisked the blood away from Lacy's lip.

"No, just listen! He said he didn't put anything in her drink, and I insisted he did, then I got him really mad, and he slapped me, and Connor saw, so he and his buddies came over and started a fistfight. That's how this happened to me." She gestured to her lip. "So then when people started trying to break up the fist fight, a food fight started. That's when I ducked out in the middle of it all."

"This just proves our theory right," Cassandra spoke up. "Zach is the monster."

"So what are we going to do?" McKenzie sighed. "If you count the teachers and that girl Garret bumped into in the hallway, not to mention all the girls Zach's already poisoned who haven't gone missing, we're so outnumbered."

"You think, McKenzie?" Kristine asked sarcastically.

Suddenly, Kristine cried out in pain and doubled over. TJ, Cassandra, McKenzie, and Lacy all rushed to her side and eased her to the ground. "What's wrong?" Cassandra wondered.

"I feel like I just got stabbed in the stomach!" she cried.

"Why?" McKenzie asked.

"If I knew, I'd tell you!" Kristine screamed.

TJ looked at his watch. "It's twelve o'clock. The nurse should still be working. Let's go."

They all started to ease her up from the floor when Cassandra's hands started to shake. All eyes turned to her.

"What's wrong?" TJ shot.

Cassandra's eyes were fixed on Kristine's hands, which were clutching her stomach. "She's bleeding," Cassandra croaked.

They all turned to Kristine's hand, which had blood trickling through the cracks where her fingers met. All of the sudden, Kristine collapsed. They all gathered around her.

"Kristine? Kristine?" TJ violently shook her arm.

"I'll get the nurse," Cassandra announced.

"Wait!" McKenzie felt for Kristine's radial pulse. "She's dead."

CHAPTER THIRTEEN

"She was cursed?" Dr. Culbreth verified.

"More like hexed," the nurse explained to the teachers and dean. They were in a small room in the back of the infirmary where students who were in-patients changed into their normal clothes after being discharged, but today, it was used for Kristine's autopsy. The nurse had determined that someone had used magic to kill her. They had used a hex to impale her somehow, very slowly and painfully.

"See here." The nurse pointed to the area around the entry wound in Kristine. "Had her murderer been standing within ten yards, there'd be burn marks around the entry wound."

"She was hexed from a distance?" Ms. Lindsey clarified.

"Yes." The nurse nodded.

"Don't allow *any* of the children to see her before tomorrow, and even then, check with us *before* letting anyone see her. Don't tell anyone about how she died. Keep everything about Kristine confidential," Dr. Culbreth ordered.

"But they have a right to know—"

"And stop being so nice to the kids," Dr. Culbreth asserted.

Ms. Edwards opened the door to the room and found that TJ, Cassandra, and McKenzie had been squatting down with their ears pressed against the door. "I just remembered!" Cassandra cried. "I forgot to put my contact in this morning."

All the kids turned to Cassandra as if she had just said, "I was just looking for a water nymph!" Everyone knew that wizards didn't need contacts. "Come on, guys," she muttered, and they all raced back to Julie's bedside, which had a curtain drawn around it because she was changing back into her uniform. The nurse had told she could leave about ten minutes before she corralled all the teachers into the back room.

"Well?" Julie pressed. You could tell she'd been crying over Kristine. She had been her roommate, and now she was gone. She felt like all those kids whose roommate's had been kidnapped, but worse. Because all those kids still had hope of seeing their roommates, as far as they were concerned, their roommates could still be alive somewhere. But Julie knew, and her friends had seen. Kristine was dead. Her body was lying on a cold slab in the back room.

"She was hexed," McKenzie reported.

"By whom?" Julie pleaded.

"Don't know," TJ answered. "All they know is that someone hexed her from a distance."

"A distance?" Julie put her face in her hands. Then she looked up and sighed. "That could be anybody!"

"We know who it isn't," TJ assured.

Cassandra looked behind them and saw the adults scowling at them. "Let's go." She put her hand on Julie's shoulder, and the four of them left. They met Morgan in the hall.

"Well?" he snapped in a hoarse voice.

"Hexed from a distance," McKenzie explained only to be ignored by Morgan. He still didn't trust Cassandra or McKenzie.

TJ had tried to convince him they were trustworthy, but Morgan disagreed. TJ had insisted a dozen times already that if they were willing to go through that mess of enrollment records just to find Julie, who wasn't exactly someone most people would want to find, then they had to honestly want to help end this crud. But Morgan just said, "The teachers could have hired them to spy on us to see what we know. They could have told them our names and gave them the locket after taking it from Qwin when they kidnapped her and told them what to say and where to be during TJ's flying lessons. For all we know, they could have hexed TJ's broom so it would go flying through the school."

TJ had to admit he had a point, so he agreed that Cassandra and McKenzie would not be invited to their secret meetings, and they would try to lead the two of them off track whenever they seemed to be getting too close to what the kids were doing, which was spying on the teachers and stealing from the teachers' private library in the back of the public library behind the false wall.

"Hexed from a distance isn't good enough!" Morgan snapped at TJ. "That could be anybody!"

"I'll tell you what I told Julie," TJ muttered. "We know who it isn't." And then he whispered so Cassandra and McKenzie couldn't hear. "Including *them*." He, of course, meant Cassandra and McKenzie.

"Doesn't matter. All that means is that they didn't hex Kristine. No one said that doesn't mean they aren't working for you-know-who," Morgan whispered.

"Doesn't mean that they are," TJ insisted.

"Want to tell us what you two are whispering about in hushed tones?" Cassandra shot back.

"Hold on," TJ told her. He was about to turn to Morgan again when the three girls moved forward.

"You don't trust us anymore or something?" Julie cried.

"Of course I trust you," TJ said.

"No, you don't!" Julie shouted. "I get put under one potion! And what the heck do you have against Cassandra and McKenzie?"

He could tell she was upset. "Nothing, Julie! We just want to make sure the teachers aren't eavesdropping," TJ assured her.

"I know you think we're working for them," McKenzie spoke up.

"How—" TJ couldn't finish.

"I may not be so book smart, but I sure as heck have street smarts and enough to know when someone doesn't trust me," Cassandra chimed in.

"Let's go." McKenzie sighed. She put her hands on Cassandra and Julie's shoulders and led them away.

Morgan sighed. "That went well."

Later that day TJ and Morgan were sitting in their dorm unhappily. "Well, at least we don't have to worry about them being traitors anymore."

"Julie was no traitor," TJ protested. "She's deceptive, secretive, annoying, a devil's advocate, and academically idiotic, but of all the things she is—"

"Including a pain in the butt," Morgan added.

"Including a pain in the butt," TJ agreed. "She's no traitor. And we need her. She knows Zach's methods, and she has more a reason now than ever to help us."

"And she knows the teacher's methods," Morgan admitted regretfully.

"So it's settled. Let's go make amends," TJ concluded. He started across the room toward the door that exited into the hall.

"What about Cassandra and McKenzie?" his roommate pondered when TJ was two feet from the door. He froze, unsure. It was clear neither of the boys knew if these girls could be trusted.

"Cassandra tried to save Qwin…and she and McKenzie haven't been charmed yet," TJ considered.

"We'll let them in because Julie trusts them, but at the first sign that they're not like us, they get stonewalled. Deal?" Morgan suggested with disdain. It was clear that Morgan didn't want to trust them at all, but he had to consider that not all the people they met had to be a monster. "The only problem is they hate us now."

"Well, they don't have to *like* us. We just need to convince them that we need to fight together and not against each other. And we'll explain that as soon as this is over they'll never have to acknowledge our presence again," TJ answered. "Now let's go apologize."

The two boys soundlessly tiptoed into the hallway, being careful to make sure no one was coming, for it was past curfew and the hallways and atriums were dark and ominous. The only light there was to guide them was moonlight and the occasional glimmering torch in the halls. They came to Cassandra and McKenzie's dorm first. TJ raised his hand and silently knocked on the girls' door. He would have just poofed in, but they figured that was rude and invasive; plus, it definitely didn't help their cause.

McKenzie opened the door, and when she saw the boys, she tried to close the door extremely fast but ended up hitting TJ's foot. She scowled at him. "What do you want?"

"Just to talk," TJ explained calmly.

"Okay, so talk."

"Can we come in?" Morgan pleaded from behind his roommate.

"No," Cassandra's voice suddenly became known, and she stepped in view behind McKenzie.

"Why not?" TJ questioned.

"We don't trust anyone," Cassandra spat as if it'd been obvious.

"And you shouldn't," TJ approved. "But sooner or later a teacher's going to walk down the corridor and see all four of us, so if I were you, I'd let us in."

McKenzie stepped aside reluctantly, and after a second of hesitation, Cassandra moved as well. The boys entered, and McKenzie closed the door behind them. The girls turned to face their visitors, who were looking around the dorm. It was like every other dorm, but instead of two dressers across from the beds, there were two desks.

"Nice room," Morgan mumbled.

"Please just say what you have to say and go," McKenzie begged.

"We're sorry," TJ admitted. "We were just paranoid and not sure who we could trust. You can understand that, right? And now we've thought over everything, and we realize we were wrong to be suspicious of you. We want you on our side. Please?"

"No," McKenzie answered as if it were just that simple.

"Why not?" Morgan cried.

"We don't like you," Cassandra shot back.

"You don't have to *like* us, just fight with us!" Morgan pointed out.

"Why should we?" Cassandra wondered.

"Because I think you want to save the students, and we want to save the students, and we sure as heck can't do that if everyone is fighting and bickering and picking sides! Divided we couldn't zap a horse fly! Together we have a chance! So, please, just this once, can't we work together?"

The girls were quiet for a few moments. "We'll fight the teachers, but not with you."

"Please," TJ pleaded. "We need to help each other."

"As a really old dude with a really cool hat once said," Morgan added, "'A house divided against itself cannot stand.'" Everyone stared at him in shock. "What?" he asked, confused.

"Dude, you just said something smart!" TJ cried in shock. "Well, sort of."

"Hey, I listen…sometimes." His face was red as a tomato.

"Well…" Cassandra turned to McKenzie for support.

"You guys did come looking for *us*, remember?" Morgan pointed out. "Not the other way around."

"We came looking for *Julie*," McKenzie pointed out. "Speaking of which, is she fighting with you?"

TJ and Morgan just looked at each other. "We were going to her next."

Now it was McKenzie and Cassandra's turn to look at each other. "Why not her first?"

"You were closer."

Cassandra looked to McKenzie, who took a certain interest in her feet. After a moment or so, she muttered, "We'll fight with you, but only until this is over. Then it'll be like you never existed. Deal?"

"Deal," the boys said in unison.

A few seconds later they were back in the hallway looking back and forth, being more careful than they'd thought possible. The last thing they needed was to run into a teacher. They were sure that would spell their doom. Every now and then, they would think they saw a teacher or a student or even Zach himself wandering the halls, but it was just a shadow or the reflection from the moonlight shining on something. After fifteen minutes or so of tiptoeing, they reached Julie's dorm. TJ knocked on her door very softly. No answer. He tried a little harder. Nothing. He tried one more time.

"Who's there?" Julie's voice called out loudly. The boys jumped and looked down the passage to make sure that no one was coming.

"It's TJ," he whispered attentively. "Can I come in?"

"No," she called out louder this time.

"Are you trying to get us caught?" Morgan accused.

"Yes!" she shouted.

"Come on, Julie," TJ pleaded. "We're on the same side!"

"Are you sure?" Julie asked sarcastically.

The boys could see that just getting to talk to Julie was going to be a challenge. "I'll give you a hundred dollars if you open the door!"

"You don't have a hundred dollars," Julie pointed out.

"Yes, I do!" he objected.

"Prove it," she ordered.

"How do you expect me to do that if you won't open the door?" he cried.

"Slide it under the door," she suggested.

TJ pulled his wallet out of his pocket and pulled out a hundred dollars. "Where'd you get that?" Morgan questioned, shocked. "With that much cash, we could have found a town and hopped a cab to the airport!"

TJ slid the money under the door. "And how do you expect to pay for our tickets?" he shot. Then to Julie, "There's your proof! Now open the door!"

Someone behind TJ and Morgan cleared her throat. The boys turned around and jumped so high they nearly hit the ceiling, for there stood Ms. Lindsey.

"We have to go to the office now, don't we?" Morgan groaned.

She nodded. "Let's go." She grabbed them by their collars and dragged them away.

They were dragged down corridor after corridor until they reached the dean's office. The whole time TJ was thinking, *How are we going to get out of this one?*

"Wait here," she ordered after she sat them down in the waiting room and went into the office.

"This is all *her* fault," Morgan grumbled.

"Ms. Lindsey?" TJ guessed.

"No, Julie. If she'd just let us in—"

"And she owes me a hundred bucks now on top of all the money she's 'borrowed' before now," TJ complained.

"How much money have you given her before?" Morgan cried in exasperation as he turned to TJ.

Before he could tell him, TJ spotted movement in the corner of his eye. He turned his head, and to his shock, he saw a glowing white ball of gas the size of a basketball floating down the hall. It stopped in front of the entrance of the waiting room and turned toward them. It was a spirit orb or, in familiar terms, a ghost. It just hovered there staring. Morgan was still staring at TJ, waiting for an answer; he hadn't seen the orb yet. TJ tapped him on his shoulder and pointed. "Look," he whispered.

He turned and stared in shock when he saw the orb. "I…it's a ghost!"

The orb hadn't moved the whole time; it just hovered there waiting. *But what for?* TJ wondered. *And what's it doing here? Not to mention, whose ghost is that?* Too many questions and no answers. Suddenly it started to move again, drifting down the hall. TJ leaped from his seat and raced into the hall.

Morgan followed. "What are you doing?" he whispered in panic.

"It wants us to follow it!" TJ explained.

"But where to?" Morgan begged.

TJ didn't know. The orb floated around corner after corner, down hall after hall. It led them through the domelike room with the creepy mural on the ceiling and down several different corridors afterward. Finally they came to a stop in front of a familiar painting of a vampire slayer. TJ knew exactly where they were. They were outside Julie's dorm.

"Why'd it take us back here?" Morgan wondered. The boys looked around for a minute, unsure what to do or say. Suddenly the orb floated *through* the painting! "What the heck?" Morgan almost screamed.

TJ tried to move the painting off the wall only to find it was stuck in place. He slid his hands down each side of the frame, trying to find an opening between the wall and the frame. That's when his eyebrows knitted together in confusion. He turned his attention to the left side of the frame.

"What is it?" Morgan asked curiously.

"Hinges," TJ whispered with excitement. "Look!" And there they were. Polished golden hinges ran down the left side of the intricate, antique frame. TJ put both his hands on the right side of the frame, dug his nails under the golden designs, and tugged with all his might. The painting swung out and hit him in the gut. He groaned and took a step back, holding his stomach. Morgan took a step toward the hole in the wall, ignoring his roommate's gasps of pain. He stuck his head in and looked around.

"It's just like the tunnel Julie and I found in the detention room!" Morgan whispered in shock. TJ looked over his shoulder and saw a few yards down the tunnel the orb waiting for them to come on. That's when they heard the voices.

"C'mon!" one shouted.

"Hurry up!" ordered a rougher voice.

"Are you sure you found them here?"

"Only a few more turns!" Ms. Lindsey assured them.

The teachers were coming, and they'd be there in a few more turns. TJ looked at Morgan, horrified. They only had one more choice if they wanted to make it through the night without being captured more than once. "Go! Go!" TJ whispered harshly. Morgan quickly stepped over and into the wall, and TJ followed just as fast. He closed the painting behind them, and just in time it seemed, for the boys heard the voices on the other side of the three-millimeter-thick canvas of the painting that concealed their hiding place.

"I thought they'd be here!" Ms. Lindsey said.

"Maybe you brought us to the wrong place!" Mrs. Sawyer spat.

"I didn't," she returned.

"Shut up," Dr. Culbreth hushed them. "We'll get them tomorrow at the farewell ceremony for that girl."

The farewell ceremony! They'd forgotten tomorrow everyone was gathering outside the school to say good-bye to Kristine as her coffin was carried down the road to the train station where her body would take its final train ride home. That is, if the students believed the teachers. The boys looked at each other's pale faces with concern in the dim white glow of the orb.

"What are we going to do?" Morgan whispered in fear. It was a good question that TJ did not know the answer to.

"For now, follow the orb," he answered. They turned and saw the orb had started to drift again. The walls were made of uneven, rough, gray bricks, and the floor was dark cement that was 75 percent covered in large, freezing puddles. Water dripped from a mysterious ceiling that was too high up to see. The orb led them down one tunnel then another. Made them turn right and then left through a labyrinth of poorly constructed tunnels. It got to the point where Morgan was sure there was no end, and TJ figured they'd never make it back to the painting without getting hopelessly lost. Finally, after what felt like hours, they reached a point where the walls got narrower and became aluminum, as did the floor and roof. Soon, the boys were on their hands and knees crawling through something extremely congruent to an air vent.

"Where is it taking us?" Morgan asked desperately.

"I don't—," TJ stopped midsentence. The narrow tunnel had ended at a grate that looked exactly like an air vent. TJ squinted, trying to see past the grate. He did his best to hold back a sneeze; the vent they were in was caked in dust. Once he wiped the water out of his eyes, he looked again. On the other side of the grate was a medium-sized room with metal rungs sticking out of the walls, like the kind used to chain prisoners to in dungeons. There was a brick fireplace at the end of the room on the back wall and an air-locked door on the right wall in the far side of the room.

"What is this place?" TJ wondered aloud. It smelled like there'd been a thousand recent fires burning in this room, and he was suddenly overcome with a waiting sense of dread. They started as murmurs, then they rose to frightened whispers, saying, "Go!" "Leave this place!" and, "Help!" Then the boys heard a piercing scream, and they jumped back, crawling as fast as they could, trying to escape. Once they hit the cold, wet concrete tunnel, they started to sprint. They didn't know where they were going; they just knew they were going.

Finally, they stopped, hands on their knees, gasping for breath. Then the orb appeared. "Please," TJ begged it. "Take us back to our dorm!"

It started to float down one tunnel, and the boys followed. Before they knew it, they'd stepped through a painting and were standing outside their dorm. The orb was next to them, and then suddenly it started to fade away. Both boys were relieved it was leaving, but Morgan had to know. "That's where you died, isn't it? That room." It stopped fading and turned toward him. It floated up and down as if it were nodding and completely faded away.

TJ stared at that room. "What was that room?"

"I don't kn—" Morgan froze, his eyes focused on the hall carpet. "Look."

There, written in mist, floated a riddle:

A thousand and one deaths have occurred in that room,

But they shall be avenged soon.

A dungeon, a gas chamber, a cabin in the woods,

Thousands of things aren't as they should.

Burning bodies bring the scent through the vent.

Save the students, but don't fall for their tricks

Or you too will be killed by the Orecs.

CHAPTER FOURTEEN

"What do you think it means?" TJ asked. After the riddle had appeared, they had stood staring at it for a minute, and when it started to disappear, Morgan wrote it on the palm of his hand with a pen he'd conjured up. The boys were too tired to realize the pen had been a Sharpie.

"I don't know," Morgan admitted. "Look, it's been a long night, and if I were back in Boston, I'd suggest staying up all night and trying to figure it out, but since I just got led down a secret passage by a ghost to the place where it and thousands of other people died and then back again after being caught by devious, manipulative—"

"I get it. You're tired," TJ muttered. "We'll discuss the riddle at the meeting tomorrow night. But right now it's three in the morning, and we have a farewell ceremony to attend tomorrow."

The boys collapsed on their beds. "Whose ghost do you think it was?" Morgan wondered aloud.

"Like the riddle said," TJ mumbled, "a thousand people, and like we saw, one ghost. How are we supposed to know?"

Morgan groaned into his pillow. And that was the last bit of the night that Morgan and TJ remembered, but whether or not anything else happened, it didn't matter because they were fairly certain they fell asleep within the next ten seconds.

TJ's alarm clock started screeching at 6:30 A.M. Morgan grumbled something that TJ couldn't quite make out and threw his pillow at it. It made a loud *bang* as it hit the floor and kept going. "Oh, for goodness' sake!" TJ moaned. And with that, he whipped out his hand and blew his alarm clock to pieces.

"Neat trick," Morgan murmured as he sat up, rubbing his eyes.

"Thanks," TJ mumbled. "Julie taught me how to do that when we were eight. Right after she used it to zap her report card. I never understood why she didn't just change the grades."

"Because that's too much work," Morgan revealed. "And where did Julie learn it?"

It was one of those good questions TJ didn't have the answer to. He guessed he'd never thought much about it before. He was certain her dad or brother wouldn't teach her something like that that; they weren't that stupid. But they were dumb enough to leave their spell books lying open everywhere. He'd never been to her house, but he distinctly remembered her telling him that. She'd also said that's why she never had sleepovers. Ha. TJ had always thought it was because she was never at school often enough to have any friends other TJ.

The boys groggily climbed out of bed and got dressed. They were wearing black dress pants and black T-shirts for the farewell ceremony. He wondered what Julie was doing.

Julie tugged the brush through her rat's nest of hair for the third time; it was obvious she hadn't slept well. She threw her brush down irritably. "Forget this," she grumbled. She was standing in front of the mirror on her dresser trying to get ready. She was wearing a black sundress and a short-sleeved gray sweater. She had clumsily strapped on her sandals, which had two-inch heels and black beads on them. She looked okay, but she felt awful.

McKenzie sighed, picked up the brush, and put her hand on Julie's shoulder, and then she gently led her over to the bed, sat her down, and started working on her hair. They were in Julie's dorm, but Cassandra and McKenzie had come by about six thirty to make sure that Julie was getting ready and not lying in bed asleep. It was a good thing they had. When they got there, Julie was asleep, face down in her pillow. They'd done everything in their power to wake her. They'd shaken her, yelled at her, and even poured a bottle of water on her head, but it was no use. The only result was a series of moans and groans that they figured were protests. In the end, she woke up when they flipped her mattress onto the ground. They figured the only reason she got up then was because she hit her head on the side table. She was awake, but she was angry too. After screaming "What the heck?" and throwing a pillow or two, she'd gotten dressed. Now they were trying to make her hair look presentable. Today, it was not an easy task.

"Calm down," McKenzie ordered her. "You have a long day ahead of you. Save your energy."

"What energy?" Julie shot. "I spend all night having night-mares about Kristine's ghost and some gas chamber—ow!" Julie interjected as McKenzie undid a massive knot in the back of her head. "And I spend all morning getting my hair pulled by you. What energy could I *possibly* have?" she snapped.

"Gas chamber?" Cassandra wondered curiously.

"I keep having these…these nightmares about…well, I'm not quite sure. I see kids who have gone missing chained in this room, and then this green gas comes in, and when it clears…" It sounded as though she might cry at any given moment. McKenzie bent down and gave her a hug, and Cassandra sat down on the bed next to her and took her hand.

"I know this is hard," McKenzie assured, "but I'm sure they're just dreams."

If only they knew, Julie thought. When McKenzie was done with Julie's hair, it tumbled down her shoulders, shining and radiant. "Thank you," Julie mumbled. McKenzie went and put the brush back on the dresser.

"Did TJ come and talk to you last night?" McKenzie tried to drop the subject of the mysterious gas chamber and the ghost of their long-lost friend and Julie's old roommate.

"He tried to," Julie explained, "but I decided not to let him in." She left out that she knew she'd gotten TJ and Morgan caught by whichever teacher was working the night patrol last night.

"He came by our room before that and apologized and all. We told him we didn't like him, but we'd help him until this is over. Then we agreed that we'd never acknowledge his presence again," Cassandra revealed.

"Sounds like a good deal," Julie admitted, "but I never opened my door. He gave me a hundred dollars too, but I never did." Julie smiled as she remembered tricking him.

"You know, some countries would consider that theft," McKenzie pointed out.

"Then it's a good thing we don't live in those countries." Julie smiled. They all smiled for the first time in days.

Cassandra looked at the clock and sighed. They all knew it was time to go. They stood and filed out into the hall. For the first time that morning, Julie took notice of what her friends were wearing. Cassandra wore a long-sleeved, black shirt that read "McJager" across the front and a knee-length black skirt with solid black Converses. McKenzie wore a medium-sleeved, black dress with black moccasins. The trio set out for the front gates of the school. Then, for some reason, Julie had that familiar feeling she got whenever Kristine was behind her. She was inclined to look back, but when she did, she stared into the seeping shadows that were the end of the hall.

"What is it?" McKenzie asked, confused, as she and Cassandra stopped, turned around, and searched the shadows that lay behind them as Julie was doing.

"Nothing. Just a feeling," Julie lied. As witches, they had a sort of sixth sense that told them when something wasn't right. Julie's sixth sense was screaming at her now as it had been since she arrived at the boarding school, but now more than ever. Slowly, the three turned around and kept walking. They knew better than to ignore their instincts, but they did anyway and kept walking toward the front of the school.

After they left, a mysterious spirit orb floated out of the shadows and watched them go. Oh, how it wished it could speak. Then maybe it could get the Wizard Police on the phone and tell *them* what was going on. If it could, the students might have a chance.

Nathan and his father sat in their kitchen in their house in Amarillo, Texas, across from Wizard Police Officer Jackson. They had poured out everything that had happened to Officer Jackson. They'd explained when, how, and why they'd sent Julie and Qwin away and how even though Phil Lynnel had e-mailed both his daughters every week, they were just now hearing from one of them. Nathan had read him the e-mail and had told how he had hesitantly called the school, what they'd said, how he'd immediately called his father, and how he'd come home and they'd called him. Now Officer Jackson, a tall, heavily built African American man with a shiny, bald head and slight mustache sat there quietly going over everything he'd just heard.

"Well?" Mr. Lynnel asked impatiently. "What are you going to do?"

"I need to make a phone call," he answered, and then he stood up, walked a few feet away, his back to the father and son, and pulled out his cell. He dialed his partner's number. "John? Yeah, it's me. I just finished my interview with the Lynnels. Add two more to the list. Julian and Qwin Lynnel. I'll poof over pictures. See you in a few minutes." He hung up the phone and turned back to the victims' family. "Sir, I'm going to be straightforward and honest. Your daughters are the five hundredth victims of a coven of Orecs." Jackson watched the color drain from their faces. "Calm down, please. Now, they may still be alive. Five hundred kids are a lot. It takes time to drain and kill that many."

"Do you think they're still alive?" Nathan managed.

"It's likely. They've been gone only month or so. There have been kids kidnapped by these creatures who were still alive for over five months," he explained. A little color returned to the other's faces. "But," he admitted, "I wouldn't get your hopes too high. Orecs are brutal creatures who feel no empathy, which means they wouldn't think twice about killing children. They never have before." The color left again.

"I'll call you when I know more," he assured them, and with that, he vanished.

Phil Lynnel put his face in his hands. "We'll find them," his son assured him. "Well, they'll find them, but they'll get found all the same."

"Oh, I have no doubt about that." Mr. Lynnel sighed. "The question is, will it be before, or after they're dead?"

Officer Jackson stared at a wall covered in pictures of children and teenagers all kidnapped and killed by these Orecs.

"Hey," his partner greeted as he walked up next to him and handed him a cup of coffee. He was a young man of medium height, about thirty-six years old, and had just been transferred to the major case unit of the Wizard Police. He had short-cut brown hair and was sort of pale. He was also kind of good looking. He gestured to the two newest pictures on the wall, one of them a fifteen-year-old girl with short, curly black hair and the same sparkling green eyes as all wizard children. The other was a ten-year-old with short dirty-blonde hair.

"Yep." James Jackson nodded.

"If we don't solve this case soon," John offered, "we're going to need another wall."

"So a good question is, why aren't we working?" James shot.

"We are," his partner answered. "We're adding two new kids to the list, and Cathy and Scott," John mentioned the other two members of their team, "are re-interviewing some of the families, seeing what we missed."

James wanted to say, "We didn't miss anything," but with the case going nowhere fast, there was nothing he could say. "What could they tell us that could possibly help?"

"I don't know. Maybe the Orecs ran out of fake addresses," John pointed out hopefully.

TJ and Morgan knelt in the bushes outside the front gates of the school, hiding from the teachers. The front gates were giant wooden doors that had intricate carvings of medieval battles. Beyond that was an area covered in tan gravel that was the size of two arenas put together; then there was a long stretch of dirt road that went for about a mile before bending out of sight somewhere in the massive forest that bordered it on both sides. A month or so ago when this nightmare first began and there were three hundred or so kids (give or take a few), the area would have been so crowded that TJ and Morgan wouldn't have had to worry about hiding; they would have just have to stand around and be two more heads in a sea of hundreds, but now there were only a hundred fifty or so, meaning TJ and Morgan had to be extremely careful.

"If we were just going to hide, we should have stayed in our dorm," Morgan suggested.

"We're not just going to hide." TJ sounded annoyed.

"So why are we here?" Morgan pondered.

"To follow them," TJ explained.

"Who?" Morgan questioned.

"The teachers carrying Kristine's casket." TJ sounded exasperated now, and he had kind of a reason to be.

"Why?" Morgan pleaded again.

"Do you honestly think," TJ began, "that they're actually going to send Kristine's body home? Please. I bet her parents don't even know she's dead!"

"Oh, good point." Morgan nodded. "One problem, though. We can't hide for the rest of the year! How are we going to keep from being caught when this is all over?"

"If things go the way I plan," TJ revealed to them, "we won't have to hide much longer. I think I know what Qwin knew. We *all* knew. We just never put the pieces together. I just need to know a second way to get to the gas chamber the ghost showed us."

"Why would they take someone who was already dead to a gas chamber?" Morgan practically cried. TJ was really freaking him out.

"I think they also use the gas chamber as a burn room," TJ explained.

Morgan didn't ask any more questions, but he had a few on his mind. The one he just couldn't figure out was how Qwin knew. Then he heard Dr. Culbreth's voice and realized the ceremony was starting. The dean gestured for the kids to make a path in the middle of the crowd, and then four teachers emerged from the gates carrying a shining silver casket that had white and orange daisies on top. There were two teachers on each side: Ms. Edwards and Ms. Lindsey on one side and Ms. Faircloth and Mr. Sawyer on the other. They carried the casket to the beginning of the dirt road and set it down; afterward, they turned toward the crowd of teary eyes and indifferent faces.

"Would anyone like to say a few words before we wish the fair …"—Ms. Lindsey whispered the name in his ear—"Kristine! Oh, yes, that's right! Kristine good-bye?"

No one raised his or her hands.

"All right." The dean sighed nonchalantly. "Take her away." All the kids knew that in wizard tradition there were a lot more gestures that were supposed to be made, but they didn't do anything. They would have been ignored anyway. The children watched as the coffin was lifted onto the shoulders of the teachers, and then they turned and started to carry their friend away. For all those who'd known her, it felt like a bullet in the heart.

The students began to funnel back into the building until TJ and Morgan were the only ones standing in the barren entryway to heck.

"Let's go." TJ and Morgan quickly leaped from the bushes and sprinted silently down the dirt road after the pallbearers. It wasn't long before they caught up. After they rounded the first bend, they saw their teachers huffing and puffing as they carried the heavy casket. TJ and Morgan doubled back into the underbrush hoping they'd be camouflaged.

"Why are caskets so heavy?" Ms. Edwards complained.

"Because bodies are in them," Ms. Lindsey grumbled sarcastically.

Mr. Sawyer was about to make another smart comment when Ms. Faircloth cut in, "Would you both shut up! We go off road here."

Suddenly they left the road and started stomping off through the underbrush and into the woods. TJ and Morgan followed. They crossed over large hills and a stream or two. TJ recorded everything on a map he was making of the area, and he'd even drawn a compass rose in the bottom left-hand corner of the map using a compass he'd conjured up. Finally, they came to a cabin that was nestled in the trough of four separate hills. TJ flashed back to the campout and how he'd followed the smoke and found this very cabin. He remembered thinking that it was on fire and that there was a living person inside; he even remembered in great detail trying to break the door in. So many things finally made sense to TJ as he watched the teachers take the casket inside, set it down, step out, and close the door.

TJ couldn't help but get closer; he had to at least try to see if anyone was trapped in the cabin. He sneaked farther down the hill and hid behind a bush then slowly looked through the door. He hadn't prepared himself for what he would see. Six kids that he could see were chained to the wall of the cabin. Some he did not recognize, some he did, and all were students. He recognized Garret and Olivia. He sprinted from the bush, ran uphill, grabbed Morgan, and ran for it, not caring how much noise he made in the process. He was lucky the teachers hadn't heard him. He ran and ran, following the map he'd made, until they were a mile from the west garden. That's when TJ bent over, hands on his stomach, and started to turn green.

"Dude, if you're gonna throw up, don't do it near me." Morgan backed up.

TJ didn't say anything; he was too busy gasping for air.

"What'd you see?" Morgan questioned.

"Kids," TJ managed.

"Who?" Morgan emphasized.

"Three guys I don't know." TJ gasped. "Garret…and Olivia."

"No. That can't…You're wrong," Morgan accused. "You have to be."

"I'm sorry," TJ admitted as he straightened up. Morgan had tears running down his cheeks. TJ remembered when he and Morgan had just met and were still getting to know each other. He remembered how Morgan had gone on and on about how much he liked her. "I'm sorry man," TJ repeated. He put his hand on his shoulder and led him back to the west garden.

That night the kids were having their routine meeting in TJ and Morgan's dorm, but tonight there weren't just five or so people in the dorm. Every kid in the school who hadn't been charmed was there—about a hundred twenty kids in all. TJ and Morgan had to magically enlarge the room and the white board he wrote on, but the room was still too crowded. Some kids were sitting in each other's laps, some had to stand in the bathroom, and some were being stepped on. Everyone was whispering loudly. TJ, Morgan, Julie, Cassandra, and McKenzie stood in front of the white board. The boys hadn't told them anything of the ghost or the discoveries they'd made in the last forty-eight hours, but Julie suspected.

"Hey!" TJ called out over the students. They ignored him. "Hey!" They ignored him again.

"Hey!" Julie screamed. Everyone stopped talking and stared.

"Thanks," TJ whispered to Julie. "You still owe me a hundred dollars." They'd made up earlier that day, but TJ made it *very* clear that he still wanted his money back. He turned to the room that was filled to the brim with kids. "Thank you for coming. Morgan, McKenzie, Cassandra, Julie, and I have an announcement to make. We have put most of the pieces together in this mystery."

TJ waited a few seconds for the students' cheers to die down. "Now, from the moment we all got here, we knew something was wrong. And then kids started to go missing. Well, you can blame Zach Forrests and Salfira Matson for that." Again he had to wait for the talking to die down. "They were working for the teachers. They'd used belief charm they'd gotten from Mr. Sawyer to charm kids and then trick them into going into the woods with them on a path that led from the east garden to a cabin in the woods. Under the cabin, the teachers drained the kids' powers. How? Our teachers aren't teachers. They're not even wizards or witches. They're Orecs." He waited for the whispers and I-told-you-sos to die down once again. "Salfira duplicated herself multiple times every morning, and one duplicate waited outside every classroom and cast the teachers' and Zach's spells for them."

"How did we never see them?" one girl asked.

"They were using an invisibility potion," TJ explained. "That we stole."

He looked back to Julie, who held up the formula that had gotten them in so much trouble for everyone to see. Multiple people applauded the theft.

"Don't encourage her," he grumbled. "Zach is also an Orec. Furthermore, whenever the dungeon under the cabin got full, the Orecs would take the kids that had been there the longest and lock them in a poisonous gas chamber." At this, there were gasps and tears for friends that they knew were probably dead now. Several kids left the room to go throw up, lots cried out, and TJ had to wait a while for the hysterical crying to calm a little bit. "After that, they burned the bodies in the same room. Qwin Lynnel figured this out, so they kidnapped her *without* charming her. Kristine came close to figuring this out and was going to warn us, so Zach used the cover of a fight in the grand hall so he could hex her. We, Morgan and I, followed the pallbearers down the road today." This earned many strange looks, especially from

Julie. "They took Kristine's body to the gas chamber and burned it, along with five other bodies."

"Who?" Many people started screaming. "Who?"

"Three people I didn't know, Garret Hamilton, and Olivia Zeigler." TJ listened to the cries of dismay and watched the tears. He was never going into a profession that involved telling people their loved ones were dead. "Listen up, everyone. We can't change the past. We didn't know any of this then, but we do now. We can do something now. Who's with me?"

A cheer rose up from the students.

"Great!" TJ nodded. "Let's go over the game plan." He turned to the white board and wrote Group A, Group B, Group C, and Group D. He used magic to make a bigger copy of his map on the white board. "Group A, you're …" He read off a list of thirty names. "Morgan will be leading you. Your job tomorrow will be to flush the teachers out of the school and into the woods through the south exit." He circled the words *Group A* and drew an arrow from them to the square that represented the school on the map.

"After that, drive them east through the woods to a clearing here." He drew an X on the clearing in the southeastern section of the map. "Group B—Cassandra, that's your group." He read off thirty more names. "You'll meet Group A in the clearing with the Orecs, and you will hold them off for as long as you can." He drew an arrow from the words *Group B* to the clearing.

"Group C, McKenzie's group." He read off another thirty names. "You're with Group D, Me and Julie's group." He read off the last thirty names. "We're going here." He pointed to the gas chamber/dungeon/cabin on the northwestern corner of the map. "The gas chamber. The plan is to rescue the students there. They will have already been drained of their powers, so they won't be able to fight with us. We'll take them and circle around." He drew a line from the cabin in the northwestern half of the map. "When we get to the dirt road, we'll send the rescued kids down the road to the closest town"—he pointed to the top of the map—"where they'll call the Wizard Police and tell them everything that's happened. Group C and Group D, we'll keep circling around until we hit the clearing, where we'll all then kill the Orecs. After that, we all go to the nearest town, meet the rescued kids, and wait for the Wizard Police to say we can go home. Any questions?"

Tara raised her hand. "How will our group leaders communicate if something doesn't go as planned?"

TJ dug into his pants pocket and produced a portable communications portal like some of the ones the teachers had. "All the group leaders will be carrying their communication portals."

"Our portals don't work!" a boy yelled. "We already tried calling the Wizard Police and our families weeks ago!"

"They cast a spell so we couldn't call our parents or the Wizard Police," TJ explained. "They didn't do anything so that we couldn't contact *each other*."

"Wait," Julie interrupted. "Can e-mails go through?"

TJ and Morgan looked at each other. "We never tried." They looked out over the crowd of kids. "Did anybody try e-mailing anyone outside the school?" No one spoke up. Julie hadn't thought many people would; a lot of magical kids had e-mail accounts, for the same reasons as Julie and Nathan, but Julie hadn't expected anyone else to attempt to use them. Anyone they knew who could help was for the most part an adult; Julie was the only person she knew besides Cassandra who didn't have all her brothers or sisters at the school, as well. TJ turned to Julie. "Did you?"

"Yeah. Nathan," she admitted. "After Kristine died, when I was in the infirmary...He never replied." It was quiet for a long time. "He didn't get the e-mail, did he?"

"Probably not." TJ was straightforward, even though he knew he should have lied. Julie's face suddenly turned even sadder then it had been before, if that was possible. "I guess that's most likely a good thing," she grumbled. "I opened the e-mail with 'hey idiot.'"

Julie had never thought she'd regret everything she'd done in her life that annoyed her brother. She never thought she'd regret acting out or stressing out her father so often, when she knew he had enough to deal with, but it was moments like this one that made her wish that maybe she been just little bit nicer to people, or that she had been an all-around better person. But she couldn't change time (mainly because there were no spells or magical objects that did so; time travel was outlawed by the Supreme Wizard Council that controlled the magical world. The reasoning behind it was that messing with the past could seriously damage the present).

TJ sighed. *Sounds like something Julie would do, all except e-mailing her brother.* He guessed she must have been desperate to go home, but she didn't want to send a message to her dad. "Okay." He turned back to the students. "We need to set our plan into motion *now* before anyone else goes missing. So is everybody in?"

The crowd let up a cheer.

"Then it's game time," Morgan said.

CHAPTER FIFTEEN

Morgan could hear the fanfare playing in his head as he came close to completing the final stop on his round. It was 7:05 A.M., ten minutes until sunrise. He turned the corner and found five members of Group A tying up the last of the water balloons in the middle of Window Lane right on top of the east exit. The plan was set to begin as soon as the sun rose. Morgan explained to his group that they would break into smaller groups of five. Three would cover the exits, and three would herd the Orecs. As the three groups chased the Orecs from the northern part of the school, the other three groups would close in, ensuring the Orecs couldn't escape through the north, east, or west exits, which would leave only the southern gate. Once they drove them out, the hard part began: herding them to the clearing. Morgan had explained to his group they would have to encircle the Orecs and lead the way. No one was a big fan of this idea. Many were afraid, and at heart, so was Morgan.

"Is everything ready?" Morgan asked as he approached the three girls and two boys. They had a flying carpet loaded down with several dozen water balloons the kids had taken turns enchanting so that they would not be able to burst until they were thrown. The enchantment also protected the balloons from their contents; the balloons were filled with water and six ounces of hydrofluoric acid, not enough to kill, but enough to burn.

"Ready," the boys replied together and nodded. "Which group are you charging with?"

Morgan reasoned, "The next group is a half a mile away. I'll charge with your group." He glanced at his watch. Seven fifteen. He looked up and saw the golden sunlight pouring in from the windows; the plan was officially in motion. "The three north groups are charging now. They're going to drive the Orecs here, then we charge. Understood?" Everyone nodded and picked up a balloon.

All that was left to do was waiting. Five minutes crept by, then ten. Suddenly, they heard it: the screeches of pain from Orecs being pelting with acid-filled water balloons. The group of courageous yet fearful children lifted their water balloons. The cries grew louder, and Morgan knew they must be just around the corner. Then the Orecs darted in, burned, bleeding, and some weeping. They stopped dead upon seeing Morgan and his group blocking their egress route and holstering water balloons.

"Ready?" Morgan called. "Aim…" In an instant, the Orecs snapped out of shock and turned around, only to find twenty more of their former students holding water balloons high above their heads. They let out cries of dismay and bolted forward toward the hallway at the end of the lane. Morgan and twenty-five other kids followed in pursuit, hurling water balloons as hard as they could. They continued to chase them through the school. When they reached a passageway to the west wing of the school, the Orecs tried to use it as an exit, but five seventh graders who were holstering water balloons greeted them. They screeched in pain and jutted southbound as they were hit with the next round of water balloons.

"Where's Salfira?" one of them whined.

Morgan stopped dead. *Oh, crap!* he thought. *We didn't factor Salfira and Zach into the plan!* He flipped out his portal and dialed TJ and then turned white as a spirit orb when he heard: "The portal you have dialed is currently unavailable. Please hang up, and try your call again." This was not good. He dialed the portal again, same message. How could they overlook the most dangerous person on the Orecs' side? How he wished his portal could place calls!

Group A proceeded to flush the Orecs out of the school. *But that won't matter*, Morgan thought, *if the rest of the plan doesn't work.*

Groups C and D had set out for the cabin before sunrise to ensure that they got there in time to prevent any more deaths. They were hiking through the wild, overgrown forest led by TJ and Julie—well, mostly TJ. He was holding his map and compass and directing the large group on which way to go. The only *real* job that Julie had been assigned was to keep the group quiet. Not that it was hard. Everyone was so nervous that talking was out of the question. So they forged on in the morning light, silent as mice.

"TJ?" Julie whispered.

"Yeah?" he answered without looking up from the map.

"Do you feel that?" Julie's stomach had already been filled with butterflies since they set out at 6:30 A.M., but now her sixth sense was kicking in, telling her something had gone wrong. She needed to know if TJ felt it too.

He was quiet for several moments. "Yeah. Yeah, I feel it too."

"What do you think it is?" she pondered.

"We're probably just nervous. If something was wrong with the plan, Morgan or McKenzie would call us," he reassured.

"What if they can't?" she fretted.

"Lower your voice," he whispered as he made a furtive glance to the younger kids that'd be going with them. "There's no need to make them even more afraid."

Julie knew he was right, so she kept walking in silence. She wondered what Nathan would have done if he *had* received her e-mail. *He would have deleted it without a second thought*, she told herself, *and then continued watching whatever stupid sporting event he was watching. What if he knew Qwin was about to die?* She questioned herself, *What would he do? Throw a party*, she answered herself. *Face it, they've long forgotten about you.* And with that depressing thought, she sighed and forced herself forward. *But what for? For your sister*, she reminded herself. *For the only* true *family you have left.*

Ten minutes later, TJ signaled to the group to stop walking. In a light whisper, he warned, "Okay, the cabin's on the other side of this hill." He pointed to the huge, mammoth hill that lay directly behind them. "So here's the plan: we're going to spread out around the four hills. When I give the whistle, close in. Break the windows, kick in the door, and be ready to fight. Remember, we have no idea what *exactly* is on the inside of that cabin. Protect yourself at all costs. Understood?" Everyone nodded. "Then let's go."

Everyone slowly began to spread out and surround the hills. TJ could tell Julie just wanted her sister back. After everyone had time to get ready, TJ let out a low whistle. Their feet hardly made a sound as they rushed over the hills and through the bushes. Multiple kids grabbed rocks or broken tree limbs and smashed the windows as three muscular guys used their shoulders to break the door in. Suddenly they all staggered back, and TJ and Julie watched as they all pulled their shirt collars over their noses and mouths. Then the two of them recognized the gas that was pouring out of the windows.

"We're too late," someone moaned.

No, Julie thought, *not this time*. She instantly sprinted forward, along with two other kids, and before TJ could catch her, she vanished into the gas chamber. Two minutes crept by, and then five. TJ was about to go in after them when Julie staggered out, with an unconscious Qwin in her arms. The other kids came out after her, dragging two kids each, but TJ didn't notice. He raced to Julie's side as she collapsed, coughing, onto her knees three yards from the entrance to the gas chamber. Tears were falling from her eyes as she laid her sister down in the leaves that covered the ground. Julie quickly put her ear to Qwin's mouth. "She's not breathing!"

TJ instantly started performing CPR, and Julie watched in horror as her sister lay lifeless on the ground. TJ performed CPR for five minutes, and one of the kids came over and made TJ stop.

"She's gone! I'm sorry, but we can't stay here." TJ knew he was right. He glanced at Julie and saw she was crying so hard she was shaking.

"No," she sobbed, "she...she can't! S...she was alive. No!" She put her face in her hands, and one of the girls had to restrain her. TJ was so upset he brought his fist down hard and accidently hit Qwin's stomach.

Qwin suddenly jackknifed up, coughing and gasping. "What?" she managed as she looked around, disoriented. Julie wrapped her sister in a bear hug; it took Qwin all of a nanosecond to recognize her sister and return the hug. The two girls were crying tears of joy as they sat there together on the ground.

"I thought I lost you," Julie explained.

"You almost did," Qwin answered. She took one look at the clearing filled with kids and asked, "What's going on?"

They quickly filled her in. TJ asked, "Do you know how to get to the dungeon?"

"Yeah," Qwin replied as the three of them climbed to their feet.

"Then let's go," TJ ordered. Everyone started heading for the cabin, which had been airing out the whole time.

Julie took in the way her sister looked, and her hatred of the Orecs grew even stronger. Qwin's short, dirty-blonde hair was matted and tangled; the clothes she wore, which had fit her fine before, were not only torn and stained but hanging onto her sister just enough to keep them from falling off. It was obvious she hadn't eaten in weeks, and she looked like she had just gone three rounds with Muhammad Ali. Julie could barely spot an inch of Qwin's body that wasn't bruised. She swore to herself that she was going to kick those Orecs to Spain and back and then slit their throats.

They entered the cabin after TJ. It was exactly how he remembered it from looking through the air vent. A door sat directly across from the entrance. "Is that the entrance to the dungeon?"

"Yeah." Qwin nodded. TJ stepped back and kicked the door in, revealing a winding stone staircase that was draped in shadows. A wave of murmurs rose up from the darkness. "It's the other kids," Qwin explained.

TJ slowly stepped over the threshold of the winding steps and found they were dripping wet. TJ held up his hand and cast, "Light from the sun or light from the stars, no matter where you are, come forth now and assist me. Without you, I cannot see." It started as a dim glow, but it slowly became brighter until there was a beam of light shining from the center of TJ's hand like a flashlight. Then he began to descend the staircase. He made each turn slowly until he finally stepped out onto the landing. He felt around for a light switch or something but found only a wooden shelf protruding about two inches from the wall. TJ reached for it and found a watery substance covering it; he brought his hand to his nose to smell it. *Kerosene?*

After casting away the light from his hand, he conjured up a box of matches and lit one and then dropped it onto the shelf. The flames lurched around until you could see the whole room. Roughly forty-five kids were chained to the right wall, which was closest to TJ, and the front wall of the concrete room was the size of an average classroom back in Amarillo. From the looks of it, they were all in the same condition as Qwin: malnourished, filthy, beaten, and relieved to be rescued. Then something piled along the left wall caught TJ's eyes. Gold! Hundreds of bars of gold! Everyone stood and stared in amazement for a few seconds, except Qwin, who'd seen this a thousand times. She walked past TJ and Julie and the others who'd followed TJ down the stairs and started attempting to pull the chains off the prisoners. Immediately TJ and the others snapped out of their trance. "Chains of iron, steel or bronze, return the freedom you have robbed," he cast. In a flash, the chains disappeared. Qwin started helping the victims stand up. Quickly, the rest of the group followed Qwin's example and started assisting the former captives. "What's that?" TJ asked, referring to the gold.

"Its how they paid Salfira," Qwin answered. "You remember all those plane crashes and missing trains? That was them. They needed a way to pay Salfira for helping them, so they used the powers they drained to steal gold."

"And the humans who were conducting the trains?" Julie pondered.

"Dead," Qwin grumbled as if it were obvious.

They were about to help the injured kids up the stairs when TJ felt a hand being put to his head from behind. "Don't move," a female voice ordered. TJ froze and the group raised their own hands and aimed carefully at the person standing behind TJ. "Do you really want me to turn your leader into a vegetable? Lower your hands."

They hesitated as Salfira stood there, smug and confident, pointing her hand at the back of TJ's head. "Now, that's the last warning I'm giving you." The children slowly lowered their hands obediently. She put her arm around TJ's neck and pulled him back, using his body as a shield and continuing to point her hand at his head. "Follow us," she seethed as she backed toward the stairs, "and he dies."

Suddenly, in an unexpected moment of courage, Julie stepped forward. "This bold witch thinks she's good as gold, but can she halt a lightning bolt?" In an instant, a bolt of lightning shot from Julie's outstretched hand and shot Salfira backward, causing her to slam into a hard stone wall. TJ turned raised his hand in a battling stance, as did everyone else, and prepared for a fight. They would have just bolted up the stairs, but that was where Salfira had landed, and no one wanted to take a chance. They had all considered poofing out, but they had just gotten these kids back and they were *not* leaving them behind, and yet they did not have the strength to take them with them should they choose to exit that way.

Salfira was already on her feet somehow, but they could tell she was scared. After all, it was one hundred five to one. All of a sudden, though, a look of confidence spread across her face. "Shield, if you'd please, come forth and shield me." That's when a large, translucent barrier appeared, blocking Salfira from them.

Oh crap, TJ thought.

"Time for you to take the fall from which you will not get up at all!" Salfira shot a bright flash of light out of her hand; it hit a girl standing to the left of TJ after passing through the barrier. The girl collapsed on the ground, and TJ didn't have to take her pulse to know she was gone.

TJ raised his hand high. "Attack!"

Multiple spell were cast, but none of the spells TJ's army cast penetrated Salfira's barrier; however, the spells she cast passed straight through and wounded kid after kid. She seemed to be saving TJ for last. He had to get them out of there now, or else Salfira would capture them all. He looked around and saw the kids whose powers had been drained cowering in the back of the room; there was nothing they could do.

"Hey, Salfira!" TJ called. She turned to him, temporarily distracted. Julie seized the opportunity and slipped through the two-inch opening between the barrier and the wall and tackled Salfira.

Salfira dropped her hand in shock, causing the barrier to vanish. She and Julie wrestled on the ground; in a nanosecond, Julie was on top of her. Julie punched her in the face as hard as she could, "That's for my sister!" she shouted. Then she pulled out her hand and pointed it at Salfira's blood-covered face, and cried out, "Time for you to take the fall from which you won't get up at all!" That ended it all, Salfira was dead and they were free to go.

TJ helped Julie up and accessed his army. A total of twenty wounded. He addressed a group of jocks of to the left, "Help the wounded and or those who are too weak to make it up the steps."

Then they left the cabin/gas chamber and dungeon and headed northeast. "Keep your eyes open," TJ warned. "We still have one orec out there somewhere."

Fifteen minutes later, they all sat down for a rest. TJ, Julie, and Qwin sat together on a bunch of tree roots that had woven together. They had told Qwin everything that had happened since she went missing and introduced her to McKenzie, who was giving them some space.

"So what happened the night you were kidnapped?" Julie wondered.

"I was in my dorm. Lacy was spending the night in someone else's room, and I had been doodling on a piece of notebook paper. I had just realized what was going on here, why kids were going missing and all, and I was about to call you when I heard someone knocking on my door. I thought maybe Lacy had forgotten something, but when I opened the door, I saw Zach and Salfira standing there. I slammed the door in their faces and used magic to board it up, but I could hear them throwing spell after spell at my door. I knew it wouldn't last much longer. As they continued to attack my door, I tore up the notebook paper I'd been doodling on and wrote on one of the pieces, but I wasn't fast enough. I knew my door was about to break, so I took what I had already written and stuffed it in my locket, but I hadn't the time to put it on. They broke down the door and grabbed me. Those two jerks dragged me across the school, down a secret passage, and the garden. What happened out there?" Qwin stared at them curiously. "Did someone try to save me?"

Julie nodded. "Cassandra did."

"Was she hurt?" Qwin questioned.

"She just got hit over the head pretty hard. Her broom was zapped, though, but that's something money can always replace," TJ reassured.

"I remember." Qwin sighed. She didn't need to tell them what happened after the garden. That much they could figure out on their own. "Tell Cassandra I said thanks for trying," she said to TJ. After several moments of quiet, Qwin admitted, "I don't have my powers anymore. They took them."

"We know," Julie replied.

"I'm not getting them back, am I?"

"Unfortunately, we can't force them to give you your powers back," TJ informed sadly. "So probably not."

"They gave Julie's powers back," Qwin protested.

"That was when they were trying to trick us into thinking they were wizards," Julie recalled. "I'm sorry, Qwin. I really am."

"I need some air," she muttered, and then she got up and walked away.

"I'm going to kill those Orecs," Julie swore through gritted teeth.

"Don't worry. We will," TJ assured.

"And then what? Go back to Amarillo? Continue to learn magic while my sister sits on the sidelines? It's not fair."

"It never is," TJ agreed, "but Qwin can still have a good life. It'll just be a *normal* life. You know, college and all."

"I love her, TJ, but could you picture Qwin getting into college? The girl broke her teacher because she couldn't think of an alternative way to not get an F."

"That was before she had a reason to care about human classes," TJ reminded.

"And she does now?"

"Now," TJ agreed, "because she doesn't have anything else."

Julie knew it was true, but she still had an urge to punch TJ in the nose. "We should get going," Julie suggested as she stood up. TJ didn't object; he gathered up the group, and they continued on.

Soon they reached the dirt road where they said good-bye to the now defenseless kids and forged on to the clearing. Julie watched her sister go on with the others, wondering if she was going to survive her battle with the Orecs long enough to see her again.

CHAPTER SIXTEEN

The hike to the town flew by without any unexpected surprises. Julie was almost disappointed when they reached the town without Zach jumping them; she wanted to kill him herself, but he didn't show. Thankfully, however, the Wizard Police did show up.

They were at the edge of the town, waiting for the cover of darkness so that they could enter the battle without the Orecs noticing, as standard procedure insisted they were supposed to do. The police were relieved at first when the kids showed, but that changed after they did a head count. Apparently, Qwin hadn't mentioned just how many kids had died in the past month or so. It was a long process. First, all the kids were looked over by wizard emergency response teams, treated for any injuries, and then they had to give detailed statements to a team of detectives who had been assigned the case of the Orec coven.

Once that was all over with, the detectives compiled a list of which kids had died and started making phone calls. It wasn't until hours later when they started calling the families of the survivors. Julie stood for hours in the cool night air that night and watched from her perch on a table underneath a tent set up by the wizard ERT as kids embraced their moms and dad and brothers and sisters and then went home. They just went home, like they would just wake up tomorrow and this would have all just been a bad dream, but that would be impossible for Julie's family.

She looked down at her little sister, who had been sitting crisscross in the tall grass next to the table where Julie sat waiting for their family. Qwin's powers were gone. How was her sister's life going to go now? Would she just sit and watch Julie and Nathan practice magic, knowing she couldn't because some monsters had drained and then brutally beaten her? Julie hated the thought. Qwin didn't deserve to be reminded forever of this horrific incident every time she walked into her own home. That wasn't even the definition of a good home, but what could Julie do? So she waited on her dad and Nathan.

She had been so shocked when she heard from Qwin that when the ex-prisoners finally reached the town at the end of the road, the Wizard Police and ERT were already there and setting up and getting ready to ambush the school! According to them, a teenage boy named Nathan Lynnel had called because the Orecs had taken his sisters. At first the girls were just two more faces on the missing persons' list, but then the detectives started digging deeper and reinvestigating everything, and they realized one of the addresses the Orecs put on the pamphlets they mailed out to advertize the school *wasn't* fake!

"How did Nathan know to call?" Julie had cried in shock.

"Somehow your e-mail got through after all!" Qwin had been so excited, and Julie had been proved wrong about her family. *They* do *care*, Julie realized.

TJ walked over to her side from wherever he'd been in the darkness and sighed. "I just told Cassandra good-bye. She hasn't left yet, though. She's still saying good-bye to the few other friends she has who weren't killed."

Julie didn't move.

"Don't you want to tell her good-bye?" TJ asked.

Julie shook her head. "I just want to take my sister home."

"I'm sure these guys will start calling Amarillo soon," TJ comforted

"I sure hope so," Julie whispered.

Just as she said this, a familiar voice called out over the crowd. "Julie? Qwin?"

Julie was on her feet in seconds. She shook her sister awake and answered, "Nathan?" The crowd of kids that were swarming under the lit space under the tent where all the kids had been waiting parted. "Dad!"

Julie and Qwin rushed forward and nearly tackled their dad in an attempt to hug him. Julie never cried, but that night, she sobbed with joy into her dad's shirt. "I promise," she vowed, "I'll never get in trouble at school again!"

"No hug for me?" Nathan laughed. The girls turned to him and nearly plowed him to the ground as well.

"I'm so sorry I called you an idiot," Julie apologized. "I thought, 'What's the point? He's not going to call.' I didn't know..." Her voice trailed off.

"I'll be honest." He sighed. "I actually missed you guys a little—a *little*." Nathan would never actually tell them he cried when he thought the only time he'd ever see his sisters again would be to identify their bodies.

Qwin nervously turned to their father, even more tears sliding down her face, "I...I'm sorry. I didn't mean what I said in the car! I know Mom cared. I know she didn't walk out on us. She loved us! I-I was just mad and confused..."

Phil Lynnel wrapped the sobbing child in a giant hug. He kneeled down and held her away from him by her shoulders so he could look her in the eyes. "I know, sweetheart. I know." He looked at her with tears in his eyes for a long moment, "She did love us all. And she *was* a good person, so strong and independent and stubborn...and you remind me of her more and more each day." He hugged his daughter tight again, and they held each other for a long moment before Phil stood up. "Let's go home," Phil Lynnel said as he embraced all three of his kids.

Qwin looked up at him with tear-filled eyes and managed, "They drained my powers. I'm not a witch anymore."

Mr. Lynnel let out a sigh. "Somehow I get the feeling you're better off."

Julie turned toward the tent one last time and waved good-bye to McKenzie, Morgan, and TJ. Then Phil Lynnel teleported his family home.

From the darkness of the trees, a ghost waved good-bye as well just before she finally went to heaven—the ghost of Julie's ex-roommate.

But someone else was watching Julie leave from the shadows. Zach Forrests swore under his breath as she disappeared into the night, "You'll pay for this. You'll pay."

The end